PROTECTION

2015, TWB Press
www.twbpress.com

Protection
Copyright © 2015 by Lane Cohen

Edited by Terry Wright

Cover Art by Terry Wright

ISBN: 978-1-936991-88-4

Acknowledgements

Many thanks to my readers along the way: Karla Jay, Karen Gail Treece, Linda Cordes, Bill Parker, my brother Ed, and the continuous encouragement of my family.

Dedication

Oh, he's got four legs and a tail,
he's got two big floppy ears,
he's got black-and-white spots all over his legs, and
he's…our bestest friend.

Chapter 1

PROTECTION, KANSAS, a sleepy town of five hundred souls set on the American prairie, was established in 1884. Its only claim to fame came in 1955 when the National Polio Foundation made its vaccine available to the residents for free. The entire town became one hundred percent protected. Other than that, Protection was a place where nothing ever happened. And so it seemed on a cold Sunday evening in November, as folks sat in front of their televisions watching NFL football, the town's reputation of serenity and boredom would continue unabated. However, unbeknownst to everyone, a lone figure, small in stature and bundled against the cold, trudged through the snow on a course that would soon pit the townsfolk against every nightmare they'd ever dreamed.

It was an old Japanese man who braved the cold

that fateful day. His hooded gray overcoat looked two sizes too large for his small frame, and he had strapped a long, narrow case across his back. He knocked on the front door of a house at the end of a dirt drive off Walnut Street. A light shown in the window, and in the driveway sat a snow-covered jeep that appeared to have been stationary for a long time. One tire was almost flat.

He waited.

The door opened. A man appeared in the doorway. Toby Gates was thirty-four years old, just over six feet tall, solid in the chest and tight around the middle. He wore faded blue jeans and a blue flannel shirt. "Evening, sir."

"Mister Gates?" The Japanese man's breath puffed in the chilled air.

"Most folks call me Toby. Can I help you?"

"I hope so, Mister Gates."

Toby looked to the street, saw no car, only footprints in the snow. "Did you walk here?"

"I don't drive. Walking gives me time to think."

A small black-and-white dog greeted the Japanese man at the door. The dog barked once and wagged his tail.

"Don't mind Jesse," Toby said. "He's my momma's dog. He won't do you no harm."

"Where is your mother?"

"Cassandra, she's in a Wichita rehab center. I hope you didn't come all this way to see her."

"I have come to see you." The man rubbed his gloved hands together. "Might I impose for some tea?"

"Depends. What's in the case strapped to your back?"

"A Samurai sword passed down from my ancestors."

Toby grimaced. "Why do you carry a Samurai sword?"

The Japanese man pushed his hood back and ran gloved fingers through his thin hair. "It is hard for me to speak the words. I-I am afraid, Mister Gates."

"Afraid of what?"

"A power much greater than us mere mortals can comprehend. The tea will be nice while I explain."

"Hot tea?"

"Yes. I am very cold."

Toby decided to be hospitable to an old man on a cold evening and moved aside. "Please, come in."

His visitor stepped into the modest two-story brick house and inhaled the spicy aroma of chili. "I am Sho Tagawa."

Toby closed the door. "May I take your coat,

Mister Tagawa?"

"Thanks, but I won't be staying long."

"There's a chair." He gestured to a weathered mud-brown recliner. "Make yourself comfortable."

A large tabby cat sat atop the back of the chair.

Tagawa removed his gloves. "Will your cat mind?"

"Nah. Not Mister Jumpers. He don't mind nothin'."

Tagawa shuffled to the chair and eased down into the cracked leather while holding the sword case upright. The tabby cat jumped to the floor.

Jesse, tail wagging, planted himself beside the new guest and sniffed at his pant cuffs.

"I'll get the tea." Toby left the room.

Tagawa inspected his surroundings. The sofa across from him was draped with a faded denim slipcover. Two denim pillows lay on the scratched wood floor, and an elk head was mounted on the wall above the sofa. Several creased gun magazines lay strewn on a knotty pine coffee table along with an open bag of Fritos. Heat radiated from a nearby wood stove. A big screen television sat in the far corner, the football game's sound muted. There were no signs of a woman's presence in the house.

Toby returned holding a mug with *Jayhawks*

written on the brown porcelain. He handed it to his visitor. "I've seen you at the bank."

Tagawa warmed his hands on the mug and sipped the tea. He settled back a bit. Jesse jumped onto his lap.

Toby sat on the sofa. He held a bottle of Boulevard lager and stared at the Japanese man.

Tagawa stared back, then: "I have seen you at the bank, as well."

"I work every day...'cept Sunday, of course. Like today."

Tagawa absently scratched Jesse's neck. "I've noticed your gun at the bank. I've often wondered, have you ever had to..."

"Shoot somebody?"

Tagawa nodded.

"No holdups here in Protection. Not since me and Stink been working there."

"Stink?"

"My younger brother."

"The large gentleman?"

"Yep." Toby took a swig of his beer.

"Odd name."

"His real name is Morgan, got his nickname when he was a kid, thought he'd chase a skunk to keep it for a pet. You can imagine the rest."

"Your brother carries a similar gun, right?"

"Yes, but we only shoot them when we go hunting from time to time. Elk and such."

"Hunting with a pistol?"

Toby gestured with his beer bottle to the mounted elk head. "Gotta be careful hunting with a Ruger Super Redhawk Alaskan. Aim wrong and half the good meat gets blown to hell."

Tagawa wiped a coat sleeve across his eyes. "You and Stink seem able to take care of yourselves."

"We look out for each other...and Jesse too, since our momma's been gone."

"Family is everything."

"Mister Tagawa..." Toby took another swallow of beer. "What power are you afraid of?"

"I have never felt such fear." He shuddered.

"That doesn't answer my question."

"It's hard to explain." Tagawa edged forward. "Will you come to my home with me? I will show you."

Jesse jumped to the floor, tail wagging in anticipation.

"Your home? When?"

"Now. It will be dark soon." Tagawa squeezed his eyes shut and sipped tea as if it was heaven-sent then opened his eyes. "What do you say?"

"Where do you live?"

"The Darabont Estate."

"On Road 3. Right? Out near the cemetery. That old place has been empty for as long as I can remember. How long you lived there?"

"I moved in four months ago. Spent my days preparing the servant's quarters for Haya while she recuperated from an illness at Evergreen Gardens in Wichita."

Toby brightened. "My momma is there now. Maybe they know each other."

"Perhaps, but earlier this month our daughter brought my wife here to live in our new home."

"So they're at the Darabont house now?"

"No. My wife, Haya, sits in a wheelchair. My daughter, Kasumi, is with her at the Prairie Motel."

"Out on Highway 160?"

Tagawa nodded.

"Why?"

"We cannot live in the house as we planned."

"Because you are afraid?"

"Yes."

"Protection's pretty quiet, Mister Tagawa. Nothing too frightening I've seen, 'cept an eighty-year-old lady trying to park her station wagon once."

"The fear is cause enough for me to carry this

sword. Kasumi carries her own sword as well, but I'm afraid they won't be enough protection against the evil in that old house. We need you to come...and bring your gun, and your brother, and his gun."

Toby didn't like Tagawa's plan at all. There was football to watch and chili-cheese Fritos to munch on, and *60-Minutes* after that. This was his day off, it was cold outside, and besides, Stink had the only car with a good battery. Toby and the old man would have to walk back to the Darabont place. That was not happening today. "I'm sorry, Mister Tagawa, I'm not interested in going to your house, with or without my gun."

Tagawa glanced around the rustic room then studied Toby. His clothes were faded and threadbare, his boots scuffed, and he wore no rings or fancy watch. And there was that broken-down jeep in the driveway. He seemed a simple man with simple needs, probably worked at the bank for minimum wage, so money could be a great motivator. "I will pay you, Mister Gates"

Toby hadn't seen that coming. "Interesting, but—"

"Here." Tagawa reached inside his coat pocket and pulled out a fist full of cash. "How about a thousand dollars?"

"A thousand..." Toby couldn't pull his eyes from Tagawa's fist full of cash.

"Five hundred for you, five hundred for your brother."

"But...five hundred dollars to walk with you from here to Road 3?" He wanted to make sure he had the details right. That was a lot of money to walk six blocks with the old man, even if it was cold outside. "Are you sure?"

"And you must look around the house so you will know my problem."

"I don't think—"

"I can get more. I will go to the bank tomorrow if this money is not enough."

"Sounds plenty but..."

"And your brother, does he live here?"

"Yes, but he ain't available."

Stink was taking a weekend class at the KSU extension, not so he could get smarter, but so he could sniff up Emma's skirt. She was the teacher and he was smitten.

Still, how hard would it be to look through an old house and tell the old man he had nothing to fear? Five hundred bucks could get him a new battery for the Jeep and maybe a tune-up and tires and...*shit*...he didn't want to blow getting five hundred bucks because Stink wasn't around. "We don't need him. I can take a look around myself."

Tagawa stared at him. "I pray to the morning sunrise you are correct."

Toby set down his beer. Foolish old man. No need to take the Alaskan. Nothing to worry about that might be dangerous in Protection on a cold evening. Besides, he had his trusty Rambo knife he always carried on his belt, and he'd be back long before sunrise.

Chapter 2

THE CHILL IN THE AIR rushed around Sho Tagawa and Toby Gates as the sun sank to the horizon. They walked side-by-side down Avenue M and approached Road 3. Jesse trotted at Toby's side. The few streetlights in Protection had not yet switched on.

The old Darabont property emerged from the growing shadows. Windbreak trees, long ago planted behind the mansion, melted into an icy fog. A flock of crows slipped effortlessly into the deepening gloom. Tagawa and Toby stopped at the long, uneven concrete walkway that led through two ancient brick columns toward a crumbling porch. Dirt-coated windows looked down on them like the weeping eyes of an old woman.

Jesse started a low growl and stood with one front paw tucked beneath him.

"Your dog should have stayed behind," Tagawa said.

"Don't need to worry about this fella. He'll stay out of trouble." Jesse wore a red sweater Toby's momma had knitted for the little guy last winter, before she got hurt.

Tagawa studied the small dog. "*Inugami*."

"What?"

"Should your dog attempt to protect you, Mister Gates, no matter his powers, he might not think about keeping himself safe."

Toby wondered what powers the old man was talking about, and if he might have more than one screw loose.

Jesse continued to growl.

Toby followed the dog's gaze. He had his eyes fixed on the sprawling house. Not a flicker of light came from the mansion windows.

"Big place for two people," Toby said.

"Three." Tagawa shivered. "Haya, Kasumi, and I occupy the servants' residence in back. This main house is empty. When I saw the online photos and considered the reasonable asking price for a home so large, my plan formed instantly. I would ready the servants' residence first, and then spend countless joyful hours refurbishing the main house. I planned to include a Bonsai garden on the grounds. Mister Gates, it would have provided endless hours of peace and enjoyment."

"I'm guessing that hasn't worked out."

"Let's go inside. I will show you why."

Tagawa stepped onto the concrete walkway. Toby followed him around back to the servants' residence, a compact one-story wooden structure. Bright light streamed from every window. An enclosed wooden atrium connected the servants' quarters to the main house. Tagawa took keys from his jacket pocket and unlocked the front door.

"Is that it, then?" Toby asked.

Tagawa's eyes watered from the cold. "Is what it?"

"I look around and then I can have my five-hundred dollars?"

"It is not going to be that easy, I fear."

"Why not?"

"Do you have your gun under that coat?"

"No."

"Why not? I told you to bring your gun."

"I don't need my gun. It's an empty house."

Tagawa seemed to deflate. "If you insist, Mister Gates. Come inside with me. But do not say I didn't warn you."

Toby thought about asking Tagawa to call him Toby once again, but changed his mind. First names didn't seem to stick with the old man very long.

Tagawa's lips pulled tight. He pushed the door open. Light spilled out everywhere.

Toby remained still. Jesse stood beside Toby's leg.

"You first, Mister Gates."

Toby looked down at Jesse, who returned his gaze. The dog's tail was wagging. Back home, NLF football and a pot of chili were waiting for him to finish with this foolishness. He took a few steps into the front room.

Jesse followed.

When everyone was inside, Tagawa closed the door.

Jesse sniffed the air.

Tagawa remained still and alert. "Seems quiet."

"Something you expecting to hear?"

Tagawa pulled the sword from its case. "Follow me."

Toby stood there, suddenly anxious, pulse rising. "Why do you need the sword in your hand?"

"I feel safer this way, Mister Gates."

Toby shrugged off an instinctive urge to draw his knife, just in case the old man wasn't crazy after all.

Tagawa stalked through the front room. It was nicely dressed in furniture and décor of Japanese design. Each porcelain knickknack was neatly in its place.

Toby and Jesse followed Tagawa a few steps behind. They angled slowly to a hallway. Every space was brightly illuminated from lamps and overhead fixtures, casting no shadows.

Tagawa glanced nervously from side to side.

Toby looked down at the floorboards. The walls in the front room and the hallway were lined with jaw traps, wire-cage traps, and snap traps. "Having a rodent problem, are you?"

Tagawa stopped and turned back to him. "I wish that were the case."

"Rats and me ain't never gotten along, but Jesse likes to chase them."

"Not rats, Mister Gates. And your dog won't be chasing these."

"Rodent problem this big, even a truckload of feral cats wouldn't do the trick. Where'd all these traps come from?"

"Benning's Hardware. I bought every one he had. All sizes, rats, mice, even skunk traps." Tagawa turned back around and began walking again.

Toby said, "Jesse. Come up here, boy."

The little dog jumped into Toby's arms and draped his front paws over Toby's shoulder. "Need to keep your nose away from all those traps."

Tagawa stopped at the end of the hallway. "This room was our last refuge." He pulled the door open.

Chapter 3

TOBY TOOK A QUICK look around. The room was ordinary. A bed, covered in quilts and pillows with oriental designs, rested against the wall near a window. A wooden rocking chair was placed just across from the bed near a table with a reading lamp. A modest dresser sat against a wall opposite the door. Small tables hugged either side of the bed.

And all the lights were on.

After his quick glance, Toby noticed a few things he typically wouldn't have seen in a bedroom. Pillows and stacks of books were set on the carpet, apparently to block the space between the floor and the bottom of the entry door, and rodent traps lined every inch of the floor at the base of the walls.

Tagawa shuffled to the rocker and sat. He drummed his fingers on the top of his knees. "I expect this must look strange to you."

Toby placed Jesse on the bed. "Stay, Jesse." Then he sat on the bed next to him and sighed. "What's this all about? Tell me why you got a hundred varmint traps set along the floorboards."

Tagawa leaned forward in the rocker. "Monsters really do live in the shadows, Mister Gates."

"I don't believe that."

"You will..." Tagawa paused as if to sort out memories in his head, then: "When I was small, I shared a bedroom with Hotaka, my older brother by two years. Hotaka cared about me, but older brothers inevitably haze their younger brothers with seemingly endless cruelty."

"I never picked on Stink even though I was two years older. Maybe 'cause Stink grew so fast and got bigger than me."

Tagawa took a long breath. "Hotaka would read stories to me from picture books at bedtime. Many times the stories were about the gunfighter heroes of the American West. Doc Holliday, Bat Masterson."

"Stink and I argue about who was the best gunfighter, Doc Holliday or Wyatt Earp."

Tagawa blinked. "Not all of Hotaka's stories were so benign. Once each year the tales were upsetting."

"How so?"

"He read to me about monsters, Mister Gates."

"Like Godzilla?"

"I would have laughed."

"Yeah, Godzilla is overrated."

"These were tales of the Obake, hideous shape-shifters, or the Jikininki, ghosts who eat humans, and the Satori, ape-like creatures who can read minds and fill children's sleep with nightmares. These monsters lurked in the shadows and waited for little boys to wander close by. One terrible night each year, these monsters became real and I could barely sleep."

"Brothers can be cruel to each other, no question, but all kids fear monsters in the closet and under the bed. You're no different, I'm sure."

"My mother told me to ignore my brother's horror tales."

"So what's your point?"

"My mother was wrong," Tagawa whispered. "And I can prove it."

Toby rolled his eyeballs. "How?"

"Everything was fine when I moved in here, but beginning this month of November I began to hear noises."

"What kind of noises?"

"At first, I thought it was my imagination. Scratching under the floor, over the ceiling, like rats in the walls. That's what I thought. That's what Haya and Kasumi thought when they joined me here."

Toby huffed. "Old empty house, rats, nothing unusual about that."

Jesse rolled over. Toby rubbed the dog's belly.

"I inspected the entire premises," Tagawa went on. "Rodent droppings were all around the basement and everywhere in the main house. I thought the critters were coming in to escape the cold, so I set a few traps, most in the basement."

"Catch anything?"

Tagawa stood and took a few steps to the dresser. He opened the top drawer and removed a large plastic food storage container. He placed it on the dresser. "Come see what I caught, Mister Gates." Tagawa removed the plastic top.

Toby joined him and peered inside, saw what looked like fur balls. "What are they?"

Tagawa reached into the container, pinched a small clump of fur, and pulled it out. "This I found in one of the traps."

Toby squinted at the tuft of fur in Tagawa's fingers. Thin tail, little feet, little claws, little ears... "Looks like a shriveled up mouse."

"Its head, body, and tail, yes, but without anything inside."

"No guts?"

"No blood. Not a thing."

Toby looked away from the dangling carcass and focused on the plastic container of fur balls. "All of them like this?"

Tagawa tipped the container over and the furry contents spilled out on the dresser. "These are just a few I collected. Dead, but fully intact, and everything drained, leaving only a husk."

"Are you saying your rats are anorexic?"

"Something is feeding on them when they get caught in the traps. After a while, the scratching stopped, and the traps remained empty. I thought the infestation was over."

Toby picked up one of the carcasses and held it between two fingers. "The trap snapped down on this one's head. Skull bones are crunched here." Its little mouth was open in frozen anguish. "Was there anything around the traps, any blood or innards?"

Tagawa shook his head.

"This collection of dead rodents don't seem enough to raise a scare."

"There's something more." Tagawa bent to the bottom drawer of the dresser. He pulled out a long, folded-over section of aluminum foil.

Jesse stared at the foil from his spot on the bed

and started to growl.

Tagawa unrolled the foil, exposing a long, furry limb.

Toby glanced at Tagawa and then focused on this new exhibit. "Holy...smokes!"

Tagawa held it up.

This new length of fur was not rodent-like at all. It was more of a monkey arm, an upper and lower part separated by an oddly jointed elbow. At the end, four sharp claws stuck out beside a stumpy node that mimicked the nub of a thumb.

Toby's stomach lurched and he had to swallow to keep from spitting up. "You caught this in one of those traps?"

Tagawa nodded. "A jaw trap. I used a dead mouse from another trap for bait."

"So whatever owned this...arm...it reached in to take the mouse..." Toby squinted at the thing in Tagawa's hand. "Where's the rest of it?"

"See this end..." Tagawa pointed to where a shoulder might have been at one time. "...how ragged it is?"

"Looks like it's been ripped off."

"I thought so at first, but after a closer look, I now believe it's been chewed off."

"The thing chewed off its arm to get free of the

trap."

"I figure it took about an hour. That's how long the tortured screeching came through the walls."

"Christ. You didn't go look?"

"Fear of the unknown is the gravest fear of all." Tagawa shuddered. "We didn't move from this room, Mister Gates. We just couldn't..."

"So whatever owns this arm is still running around in your walls? Is that what you want me to believe?"

"I want you to believe you should have brought your gun."

"How dangerous is a monkey...or whatever it is?"

Tagawa looked as though he had stopped breathing. "Two nights ago, Mister Gates, we saw one of them."

"There's more than one?"

"It was in the shadows, by the bedroom door. Just *sitting* there. Watching us. Inside the bedroom. We had left one table lamp lighted as we slept, but at that moment I awoke, when I focused on the horror from across the room, I truly wished for complete darkness."

Tagawa recalled that horror. "I was almost grateful when I saw Haya's eyes widen at the hideous creature in our bedroom. She could barely move at all, and expressions of pain, discomfort, or even pleasure were rare. But seeing that creature caused her face to contort, and she screamed and tried to push herself to an upright position on the mattress."

"What did you do?" Toby asked, wide-eyed as he imagined Haya's terror.

"I scrambled from the bed and grabbed my sword from the floor. The creature didn't move so I placed my body as a barricade between Haya and the monster. It had all four of its limbs, so I knew there were others. Kasumi rushed in with her own sword and slapped on the lights. In the brilliant glare the abomination bared its pointy teeth and hissed at us."

"You sure it had both arms?"

"Yes. And both hairy legs."

Toby's eyes darted about the room. "Then you're right. There are a nest of them in this house."

"Kasumi inched toward the thing. It was only three feet tall. I told her to be careful, her hands were shaking, but when the grotesque fiend screeched at her, she fell back...and then...and then in one swift movement the creature turned and melted into the wall."

"No way." Toby stared at Tagawa "You sure you were really awake?"

"Yes. I saw it. We all saw it."

"And it just disappeared through the wall? How's that possible?"

Tagawa curled a finger at him. "Look here." He moved to the wall, pushed on it, and a panel opened.

"A secret passage. We should go in, follow it, see where it leads."

"But you did not bring your gun."

Now Toby shuddered. He wasn't going in there without the Alaskan.

Tagawa shook a fist at the opening. "It is how the creatures move from room to room unimpeded by closed doors."

Toby gazed at the darkness behind the open wood panel. "Don't sound like no critter from around this town. Not a raccoon or possum or squirrel. Could be some kind of monkey escaped from the circus...'cept there ain't been a circus come within fifty miles of Protection for several years now."

Tagawa stepped away from the wall. "The fact that the creature displayed the intelligence to access this passageway scares me more than anything else."

"An intelligent monkey?" Toby scratched his chin. "Well, they did go into space. But a bunch of 'em? And one doesn't have an arm. No wonder you moved your family to the motel."

"The very next morning." He strode to the door. "Now you will come with me to the basement."

"The basement?" He swallowed. "Are you sure that's a good idea?"

"There is something you must hear."

Toby thought he should go home first and get his gun, but he wasn't entirely unarmed. He unbuttoned his canvas field coat and pulled it back along one side to reveal the Rambo knife fastened to his belt. He'd bought it on EBay a couple years back. Now he could get to it quickly.

Tagawa led him to a stairwell door.

Toby squinted from the brilliant light that flooded the basement stairs. "Your electric bill must be awful high."

"Small price, Mister Gates, to keep the monsters away."

He followed Tagawa down toward the cellar. Fluorescent bulbs lined the ceiling from the top of the first step to the bottom where thick beige carpet covered the basement floor. The lower level shimmered with more light than the stairway, and it was completely empty, without a single piece of furniture.

Tagawa turned to Toby. "When the noises first began, I believed they were coming from down here."

"You said the noises were coming from the walls."

"Echoing from down here." Tagawa swept a hand around the room. "This basement was dark and damp and musty, a perfect hideout for monsters, so I hired a contractor to install the lighting, paint the walls white, and lay the carpeting. I wanted no sanctuary for the hairy creatures, no shadows in which to hide."

Toby admired the stark, clean, incredibly lighted room. It was easy to imagine a pool table in the center and a wet-bar along the wall, a great place for a man-cave. But there were traps along the walls here too. He came to an obvious conclusion. "So all this renovation didn't work. Whatever's living here isn't gone."

"Follow me, please." Tagawa stepped quickly across the main basement room to a smaller adjoining area. This room would have been empty but for one metal folding chair and a small table beside it. As before, the lights in the room were blinding and traps lined the walls.

Tagawa moved to the rear of the room and placed an open palm on a thick, wooden door, also painted white. "I heard the scratching in the walls most everywhere in the house. But down here, especially in this area, I could also hear music."

Toby stared at him. "What kind of music?"

"Come over here, Mister Gates."

Toby walked up beside him.

Tagawa brought one finger to his lips. "Listen."

Toby heard the very faint echo of a song.

"Recognize it?"

Toby put his ear to the door. "*I Heard It Through The Grapevine.* He glanced around the room, and then gazed at the door. "What's on the other side?"

"I believe it is an underground passageway between the main house and these servants' quarters, but the door is locked. I asked Mister Benning at the hardware store if he could fashion a key, but he took a look and said the mechanism was so ancient he would have to research the manufacturer and get back to me."

"How long will that take?"

Tagawa shrugged.

"What about the other end, in the main house?"

"I investigated the basement there and discovered no door, but the wall is entirely made of newer red bricks, as though someone had wanted that tunnel sealed and hidden forever."

Toby had glanced down at the carpet in front of the locked door and noticed something unusual.

"Wait a minute. Someone tracked dirt through here."

"I've seen that before and always cleaned it completely. This residue is fresh."

"That means whatever came through this door is around here somewhere."

Tagawa looked around the barren bright room. "We never saw the creatures during the daylight hours. They had emerged only in darkness."

"So it's hiding in the walls. How do we get it to come out?"

"If we are to draw the monster out now, it must be dark down here." He rushed into the main room and turned off those lights, and then stepped into the backroom and stood at the wall switch. "Now you will see the horrors that have been stalking my family, and then you will truly believe that monsters live in the shadows." He flipped the switch, plunging the room into total darkness. "And you will wish you had your gun."

Toby gritted his teeth as spots of multicolored lights flashed behind his retinas in rhythm to the faint tune of *I Heard It Through The Grapevine*. He waited.

Chapter 4

MIRA GOLDSTEIN LAWRENCE didn't think she could stand being cooped up for one more day. She stood with her hands on her hips and glared across the room at her husband, Talbot, who was stretched out and smiling in his extravagant velvet lounger, as always it seemed, writing in his journal and listening to that horrible music.

I heard it through the grapevine...

"I hate this dreadful place," Mira said.

Talbot glanced up at her. "So you keep saying, my love."

"Your love? Humph."

He took a glass of white wine from a side table, raised the glass to her, and took a swallow. "Yes. I do love you."

"Then get us out of this town."

"All in good time, my love."

She dropped into a chair, pulling the bottom of her long red dressing gown out from under her legs. "How much longer must we stay here, Talbot? Months? Years? Forever?"

He smiled, punched a button on a cassette player, and continued to write in the thick leather journal.

A new song started. *Runaround Sue.*

His straight white hair fell across his forehead. "You always get like this, Mira, after giving birth. It's postpartum something or another."

"Talbot, please, turn off that music."

"I would like to finish this one page."

"More poetry?"

He smiled, not a care in the world. "I express myself this way. You know that by now."

"Why don't you express yourself like other men, play golf, shoot pool, go bowling. Then I can go shopping, preferably in New York City. There's not a single boutique in this town."

He leaned forward, his pale blue eyes glowing at her. "Would you like to read some of my poetry?" He held the ragged-paged journal out to her. It looked to be hundreds of pages thick.

She fiddled with the ends of her auburn hair, visited by an occasional streak of deep red. "What's it about this time?"

"Feelings. Thoughts. About the twins."

She looked away. "Where are those boys? I haven't seen them for hours."

"They are fine. Just fine." He smiled, opened his journal, and made another notation. "What can harm them in this old house?"

"I don't approve of letting them go around at this age, completely unsupervised."

"Mira, my dear," he said without looking up, "this is always what you say, each new mating season." He closed the journal and blinked at her. "And you have never read a word of my poetry."

"You've recited some of it to me. That was enough. Boring."

"It interests me."

"Do I interest you, Talbot?"

He grinned. "You are my eternal inspiration, my love."

She moved from the chair, glided onto his lap, and took his face in her chalk-white hands. "Then how much longer will your eternal inspiration have to spend in this lousy town?" She playfully nibbled at the bottom of his ear. "I want to go where the lights are bright and the air is scented with fine spices, and the music is anything but this old drivel you listen to."

"You know we can't do that." Talbot breathed, enjoying her loving attention. "We must keep a low-profile."

"Screw that. Let's live a little."

"That's what got us in trouble in Wichita."

"I miss the arts, the theater, the symphony. Why can't we have it here in Protection? Open up our own clubs and fine restaurants. A theater with high chandeliers—"

"We can't, so forget it, Mira."

"Pooh, you're no fun anymore."

He rubbed the edge of his pinky finger down her cheek. "You are so beautiful. I wish I could give you the lifestyle you want, but our life is what it is."

She pressed the side of her face to his chest. "Someday..."

***

Faint scratching sounds came out of the blackness. Every muscle in Toby's body stiffened. Then a rustling sound followed, louder. Closer. A snort and a grunt.

"It is coming," Tagawa whispered.

Hand shaking, Toby unsheathed his Rambo knife and braced his back against a wall. He hadn't felt this level of fear since Taliban insurgents were searching an abandoned mud-brick school in which he and his patrol had taken shelter during an attack.

The shuffling and snorting got closer.

"Prepare yourself, Mister Gates." Tagawa turned on the lights.

In the blinding glow, a hairy creature screeched and reared up on its hind legs. Toby had to blink to be sure what he was seeing was real. The thing was nightmarish, unlike any animal from these parts, and it was well protected with long black talons extending from its forearms. Its teeth in full display were tiny and pointed, all in a row, almost reptilian, and its eyes were dark and streaked with red.

"Maybe now you understand." Tagawa moved toward the monster, sword drawn.

Toby didn't know what to say, but he had no trouble thinking Tagawa had been right all along. The Rambo knife wouldn't get through all that hair much less stab deep enough to pierce the heart. This was a job for his absent Alaskan.

The monster shrunk back from Tagawa. It hunched itself into a crowded ball, its head and neck almost disappearing into a hairy, black middle, and then it rolled backward into the still dark main room.

"It's getting away." Tagawa gave chase.

Toby swallowed, thought he should stay in the lighted room, but within an instant, the adjoining room lit up, and the monster's shrieking became painful to hear.

"Please, Mister Gates, come quickly. We have to kill it now or others may come."

Toby rushed to Tagawa's side. He held the sword in front of him, hands trembling badly. Each step he took toward the creature brought more shrieking. It had pressed itself against the basement wall.

"Wait." Toby grabbed the old man's arm, his muscles tense as forged steel. "It's not attacking us...it's afraid of us."

"It is waiting for a time to strike, same as the Jikininki or the Satori who eat human flesh and fill our minds with nightmares, the monsters my brother read to me about." He jerked his arm loose from Toby's grip. "They are here in my house and are not welcome."

Tagawa moved closer to the monster of his childhood dreams, which had worked itself into a corner. Toby couldn't take his eyes off the creature. He felt repulsed, but strangely fascinated. There had to be a logical explanation for its existence. The thing could even be worth some money or worthy of the

Guinness Book of World Records for ugliness.

The closer Tagawa got to it, the more it hissed and screeched. It straightened its body to a full three feet, extended its vicious talons, and shrieked so loud Toby thought his hearing would be permanently damaged.

Tagawa flinched, held back, sword up high. Sweat beaded on his forehead. "Why did it choose my house to haunt?"

"Please wait, Sho. We should call Sheriff Lockwood."

"It is cornered now, but for how long? When will others of its kind come to its aid? I must act now or abandon all hope of living here in peace."

Jesse started barking like crazy. Upstairs.

Toby and Tagawa stared at each other.

A horrible squeal came next, followed by a menacing, high-pitched screech.

More barking and growling.

"Jesse," Toby shouted. He spun around and bolted up the stairs to the kitchen. "Jesse!" He held his knife out in front of him. His stomach twisted the instant he saw Jesse had another one of those ugly devils backed into a corner. This one was missing an arm, but it was still lightning quick as it slashed out at Jesse with its remaining arm and talons.

Jesse dodged to the side.

"Jesse, no!"

The dog glanced at Toby but quickly regained his aggressive stance and snarled at the creature.

"Jesse, get back." Toby inched forward. If only he could get his arm under the little mutt, if only he could scoop him into the air and back away, before—

The creature shrieked, lunged, and slashed out.

Jesse yelped and fell.

Toby rushed forward and grabbed Jesse under his belly.

The creature scuttled from the kitchen and down the hallway.

"Jesse?"

The dog gasped and pressed his head against Toby's chest. His little body shuddered.

Hot wetness bathed Toby's arm. He looked down and saw a blood smear spreading down the front of his canvas field coat.

Panic shot through Toby's gut as he checked the dog's injuries. Abdominal laceration. Extended intestines. His eyes went out of focus.

Tagawa appeared blurry when he entered the kitchen, holding the hairy head of the downstairs creature in one hand and his sword in the other, both dripping blood. "I got this one."

"Another one got away."

Tagawa dropped the head on the floor. "Is your dog all right?"

"Does he look all right?" Toby sheathed the knife.

"I told you that dog shouldn't come."

"I gotta go...gotta get him help." Toby took a deep breath and rushed out of the old Darabont servants' quarters and into the black cold of night, cradling Jesse close to his chest, and running as fast as he could manage back toward home.

Tears burned his eyes. He wished he'd never met Sho Tagawa. He wished he'd stayed home and watched football. Now Jesse was horribly injured, maybe dying, little Jesse who was never far from his side and who slept every night on a pillow beside his bed. Toby could never let this atrocity go un-avenged. Now he had a score to settle with those creatures, a score that demanded blood retribution, and if Jesse didn't make it, he'd burn down that goddamned Darabont Estate and piss on the ashes.

***

Screeching pierced the walls...then a dog barked from somewhere in the house.

Mira and Talbot sat straight up. "What's going

on?" she shrieked.

"The boys are in trouble." Talbot tossed his journal aside and jumped to his feet. "Stay here."

"No."

"Mira. I'm going. Only one of us at a time can take the risk of being caught out there."

She stared at him. "Be careful."

Talbot pulled up the sleeves of his dark dressing gown then straightened his arms. Smooth black talons edged out and extended through the skin on both wrists. "I'll be right back."

He raced barefoot through the shadows to the basement door. He jerked the old deadbolt, swung the door open, and ducked through the doorframe. Bright light poured across the threshold as if he had just stepped out onto the surface of the sun. He wondered what cruel sickness could have invaded the mind of the person who decided to light this basement as if it were a hospital operating theatre.

For the many years Talbot's family had occupied the house for each breeding season in November. Their home had been cool, dark, and welcoming until that pesky Japanese man moved in.

This first room, as always, contained one chair and a small table. He squinted at the brightness and struck out across the thick carpet to the next room where he spotted an odd heap in the corner, yet oddly familiar, the hair and limbs, and then he saw the blood spattered on the wall and pooled on the carpet.

His breath caught in his throat. "No. God no." He staggered across the room and knelt at the headless remains of his son. Which son he couldn't tell. "This, this cannot be."

Fearing the killer was nearby, he spun around, shielded his eyes from the glare and scanned the room again. Seeing nothing and no one else, he bent down and touched the arm of what was left of the fallen boy. Talbot's throat seized, trapping his next breath or he would have screamed bloody murder. The boy's arm was still warm, but it would grow cold quickly. And where was his head? Who took it? Who would do such a thing? Tears blurred his vision and the walls started creeping in. He didn't know which son to cry for, Evan or Ephram. Each owned his heart, and now his heart was dead. How could he tell Mira that a child from her womb had been taken in such a violent manner?

She would not take this terrible news well, and all he could think to do at this moment was run, find the killer, and kill the killer before Mira found out...

Chapter 5

MORGAN 'STINK' GATES remained motionless in his chair and gazed at Ms. Emma Naveed as she sat perched on the edge of her desk, lecturing the class from the front of the room. However, he wasn't motionless inside, the way his heart was beating at the sight of her legs crossed at the knees. She was twenty-seven years old, slim and trim, and classy, way above his pay grade.

He glanced down at his iPad every ten seconds or so, just to make it seem like he was actually paying attention to this evening's linguistics lesson.

A few months ago, Stink had helped Ms. Naveed when her car got a flat tire. It happened in front of the firehouse where he volunteered when he wasn't on duty at the bank. He remembered going out to her car and how she'd whipped off her sunglasses and stared up at him, her green eyes glistening with bridled tears. "I don't know what to do." He caught the fragrance of her scented lotion and his heart started beating in an alternate universe. "I'll take care of it for you, ma'am." He took about ten minutes longer than necessary to switch out the tires, just to be near her a little longer. And during that time, he learned she taught weekend linguistics classes at the KSU extension in Protection. Two days later, he had registered for her class.

"Class dismissed," Ms. Naveed announced. "See you next weekend."

He hoped he wouldn't have to wait an entire week before he'd see her again.

On the way home, he gripped the steering wheel of his Buick Roadmaster as he guided the huge black vehicle down the last street toward his house. The classroom was located in an old converted warehouse on Washington Street, and it was walking distance from his house, which he'd walk if the weather was nice. But it was a snowy November night, and he took advantage of the near-nuclear heat of the old Buick's heater. The Roadmaster got horrible mileage, but it was one of the few cars he could sit in comfortably.

Tonight in class, he had participated in the discussions best he could. He wanted Ms. Naveed to think he was a smart guy, and not some dumb hick who got fired from the local Salvation Army store because of mistakes he'd made working the cash register. Jobs were scarce in Protection, so he joined the army with his brother, Toby. Stink didn't know if he had impressed Emma with his comments, but she had smiled at him once, so that was enough to make taking the class worthwhile.

As he pulled the Roadmaster into his driveway, he could not get Emma Naveed out of his brain. He stopped the car behind Toby's battered Jeep Wrangler. With the motor still running and the heater still blazing, Stink listened to the end of *Feels Like the First Time* blasting from the radio. He wondered if Emma would ever kiss him —

Someone pounded on the roof of his car.

Stink flinched.

"Open the door!" Toby yelled from outside the passenger side window. He held Jesse in his arms. Blood dripped from the dog's red sweater, and his head was lolled to the side.

Stink's breathing stopped.

"Open up!"

Stink gasped and jabbed the unlock button.

Toby climbed in. "Drive." He was out of breath.

"What the hell happened to Momma's dog?" Stink shrieked.

Toby pointed out the window with bloody fingers. "Doc Barnett's. Go!"

Stink slammed the transmission lever into reverse and powered out of the driveway.

***

For the last thirty minutes, Stink had watched his brother keep dead silent and stare at the polished wood floor of Doc Barnett's waiting room. Toby's elbows were propped on his knees and his hands were clasped tight and shaking. On the way over, Toby hadn't said anything about what happened, just pressed Jesse close to his bloody jacket as if holding the dog tighter might stop the bleeding. And the look in Toby's eyes was downright frightening, something he hadn't seen since their firefights in Afghanistan, and something they hadn't even talked about since Toby started PTSD therapy sessions down at the VA in Wichita.

Doc Barnett lived upstairs above the vet clinic, and it was a good thing, since the closest full-time animal emergency hospital was at least an hour's drive away.

Finally, Doc opened the operating room door and stepped into the waiting room, drying his hands with a paper towel. He was about thirty-two years old, six feet tall, and thin-boned. He sneezed and dabbed at his nose. "Bleeding's stopped," he said in a southern drawl.

Toby jumped to his feet. "Doc, how is he?"

"How bad is it?" Stink asked.

"He suffered two deep abdominal lacerations. One severed an artery. I sutured that to stop the majority of the bleeding." He sneezed again and wiped at his eyes and mouth. "You boys have got some explaining to do. What happened to that poor dog?"

"It was dark." Toby stared at the doctor. No way could Toby tell him some creature from hell attacked Jesse. Who would believe that? And if Doc told the sheriff, he'd either lock Toby up in the loony bin or send a posse out to the Darabont estate to investigate. He didn't want that, no, those creatures were his, and he was going to kill them all if he had to take the place apart, board by fucking board.

Stink stared at Toby. "Well? You explaining or not?"

He took a breath. "Coyote, maybe."

Doc huffed. "Those were not bite wounds. Something tore into that dog with claws."

"A bear?" Stink asked.

"When have you ever seen a bear in these parts?"

"A possum?"

"What dog can't outrun a possum?"

"A sloth," Stink ventured. "They got some huge claws. What do you think, Toby? Was it a sloth?"

"Enough! I don't know what it was!" Toby's face heated with anger. Too many questions. And the truth was he didn't know. "Can I take him home, Doc?"

Barnett wiped his runny nose. "No. I had to put him under anesthesia for the surgery, and I left the incision open in case he suffers a relapse. I'll close him up in the morning. Then I'll reevaluate his prognosis."

Stink asked, "Will he have to wear one of those cones of shame?"

Toby glared at his brother. "Jesse's damn near dead and you're worried about a stupid cone? What's the matter with you?"

Doc intervened. "It's late, boys. Take it easy. There's nothing more we can do for him tonight." He sneezed again. "Go home."

"That's a nasty cold, Doc," Stink said.

"I'd have to get better to die."

Toby's feet felt rooted to the floor. He didn't want to go. He didn't want to leave Jesse, but he had to finish what those monsters had started. "I thank you, Doc. My momma thanks you. Take good care of the little guy for us. I won't forget it. I don't forget nobody who helps my family."

"Remember that when you get my bill."

"Yeah, Doc," Stink said. "Thanks."

Doc showed them to the door.

Stink and Toby walked silently to the Roadmaster. They opened the doors and dropped inside. Stink glanced at Toby's hands, still streaked with Jesse's blood. "What happened, Toby?"

Toby stared straight into his brother's eyes. "Start the car."

Stink started the engine. "Where we goin'?"

Toby made a fist. "Home."

"Mabye we should stop and get a beer, let you calm down some."

"We don't need a beer. We need to get our guns."

***

Stink stood behind Toby and watched him push six brass casings into his Alaskan. He swiveled the cylinder shut, and it locked with a solid click. "Stink. You're next." He eased the heavy pistol into the holster on his right hip.

"I don't know, man, this is crazy."

Toby reached to a shelf in the bedroom closet, stepped back out, offered another Ruger Alaskan to Stink.

He took the pistol and held it loosely in one huge hand, down at his side. "Look, I know you're upset."

"Damn right I'm upset."

Toby rummaged along the closet shelf. "Get loaded up."

"Toby, can we talk about this?"

"About what?"

"We've been back from the sand for three years now. Three years, Toby, and your PTSD isn't getting any better."

"This ain't about Afghanistan." Toby angled back out of the closet and faced his brother. "And it ain't about my PTSD." He threw a box of shells on the bed.

Stink was two inches taller than Toby, but he still flinched and stepped back. "You gotta calm down, Toby."

"You ain't my therapist. Load your weapon." Toby edged Stink aside and grabbed a handful of 454 Casull cartridges from the box on the bed and stuffed them in his pockets.

Stink remembered the last time Toby had this same crazy killing look in his eyes, and seeing it come out of the blue again was unsettling. "It's not a good idea to run around town with loaded guns."

Toby shuffled around him, back to the closet, and found a military-spec flashlight. "We're leaving in two minutes."

"Going where?"

Swollen blood vessels bulged at Toby's temples. "Darabont mansion."

"That old place?" Stink shoved shells into his Alaskan. "What are we gonna do there?"

"Did you see Jesse? Did you really look at him?"

"I saw him, I saw him."

"He was cut open, Stink. Gutted and he damn near bled out."

"I love Jesse too, Toby, but—"

"The dog was just trying to warn me and ended up..." He clenched his fists at his sides. "I can't let that go, Stink. I couldn't face our momma if he dies."

"I understand."

"You with me, then?"

"But Darabont's been empty for years."

"Not no more."

"Will you please just tell me what you wanna do over there?"

Toby fixed his stare on Stink. "We're going over there to kill us some ugly fucking monsters."

Chapter 6

SHO TAGAWA STEPPED DOWN the middle of the deserted street and tried not to think of the cold. His entire sense of balance and general orientation with the world had been left behind in the basement of the servants' quarters of the old Darabont place.

He had vanquished one of the hairy creatures in a way that honored his ancestors. The thought of that victory made him smile, even though the wind was picking up, and any warmth he had retained after leaving the house had already departed.

Headlights flared into his eyes. A huge black car edged to the curb and rolled to a stop. The passenger window descended.

"Sho," Toby called from the car.

Tagawa squinted in through the window. "Mister Gates. I was headed your direction."

"Get in. Quick."

Tagawa blinked and shuffled to a rear door, dropped his sword inside, and ducked his head to get in.

"Go," Toby said to the driver.

Stink glanced back at Tagawa and swerved the car to the middle of the street. "Why did that Chinese man drop a bloody sword on my back seat?"

"He's Japanese, Stink. Make a right turn here, and two blocks down. Toward the cemetery."

"I know where it is, Toby."

"Then drive."

"I think I've seen this Japanese guy at the bank."

"He's Mister Sho Tagawa."

"I'm Morgan, Toby's brother. People call me Stink."

"Pleased to finally meet you."

"Why do you have a sword?"

Toby said, "Mister Tagawa uses a sword from his Samurai ancestors. And apparently he's pretty fucking good with it."

"Then whose blood is on it?"

Toby looked back at Tagawa. "I think the right question is what creature's blood is on his Samurai sword."

Stink glanced at Tagawa again via the rear view mirror. "What creature's blood is on your sword?"

"A dead creature's blood," Tagawa responded.

"Slow down," Toby told Stink.

"But the Darabont house is still another block ahead."

"Stop here."

Stink slowed and stopped the Roadmaster.

"I want to approach from a fair distance," Toby said. "Ain't sure yet what we're dealing with yet."

"Look at that." Stink squinted down the road. "We got something right here to deal with. Hard to see."

Tagawa pressed his face close to the window. "It is a man."

"Damn dark out here," Toby griped.

Stink rolled the car forward till the headlights hit the man in the road. "Hell, ain't that Mayor Lawrence?"

Toby rubbed breath fog from the inside of the windshield with his fingers. "It sure is and he don't look too happy."

"Why would he be walking around alone on this cold night?"

"He is barefoot," Tagawa added.

Stink shook his head. "That can't be good. Is he drunk?"

Mayor Talbot Lawrence reached the Roadmaster.

He motioned for Stink to roll down his window.

"What are you doing out here, sir?" Stink asked him.

Talbot bent at the waist and put his hands on the roof of the car. Talbot was so tall he still had to bend his knees and lower his head to get eye-level with Stink. "I should ask you boys the same thing. Have you been inside that old house?"

Stink sized up the mayor with a quick glance. The man was six-foot-five and rangy. He looked sixty-something but was probably younger than he looked because of his white hair. It was long and straight and swept across his forehead. But the most striking feature of Mayor Talbot Lawrence was his eyes. They were pale blue and seemed to glow with an inner radiance.

Stink said, "I thought you were on your yearly cultural exchange to Bolivia. You're usually gone most of November, right, staying at that family villa?"

"We got to get going," Toby said to Stink.

Talbot gritted his teeth. "Going where?"

"Mayor, you okay?" Stink asked.

"Why? Don't I look okay?"

"Pretty cold to go for a walk at this time of night, barefoot, wearing a bathrobe."

Talbot scowled at Stink. "It's a dressing gown."

"This ain't even your neighborhood. You out looking for a lost dog, or somethin'?"

"I'm looking for my son's killer before Mira finds out and goes looking on her own."

Tagawa felt heat rush to his face. His scalp tingled. This man in the street, this tall man with hair the color of snow, this man was referring to the thing...the hairy, vicious creature...as his son? That would make the mayor a monster too. Tagawa threw open the Roadmaster door and stepped onto the weather-cracked blacktop.

"Tagawa, get back in here," Toby shouted. At this rate he would never make it back to the Darabont house and find the creature that damn near killed Jesse.

Tagawa moved around the car, his Samurai sword held down in one hand. As he approached the mayor, he lifted the sword horizontally and held it steady in front of his forehead.

Toby shouted, "Goddamn it, Sho." He jumped out of the car and rushed to Tagawa with his palms open and extended in front of him. "What are you doing?"

Tagawa's eyes were fixed on Mayor Lawrence but he spoke to Toby. "Your *Inugami*. Has your dog survived?"

"Doc Barnett stitched him up. He's alive for now."

Talbot tilted his head to Toby. "How was your dog hurt?"

Toby ventured a step closer to Protection's mayor. "Some creature in the Darabont mansion cut him with its claws. You know anything about that?"

Talbot's eyes narrowed and he edged back a step.

Tagawa inched forward. "My inside jacket pocket," he said to Toby. "Your money...it's all there."

"Money?" Stink climbed out of the car. "What the heck, Toby?"

"He's payin' us to help him with a varmint problem. Tagawa got one of 'em, Stink."

Talbot focused on the red crust that coated Tagawa's sword. "You're the one who killed him?"

"Yes."

"But why?"

"Some things require no explanation."

"Then I should not have to explain killing you."

"My ancestors would be proud to see their sword through your evil heart." Tagawa reared back with the sword.

"Wait!" Stink jumped in front of him, arms spread wide. "Whoa, there, old man. Cool it with the blade."

"I am not afraid of him."

"He's the mayor."

"He's a monster."

Stink and Toby turned to look at the mayor. "Monster?"

His face was serene, not threatening at all, as if he were about to deliver a eulogy at the funeral home. "Move aside, boys."

Stink squinted at him but did not budge.

Talbot powered his right fist around and struck Stink, who smashed backward into the fender of the Roadmaster and crumpled to the pavement.

Toby's eyes popped wide. He had never seen anybody deck Stink, and the mayor had done it so easily.

"You too," Talbot said to Toby. "Move."

"I can't let you get away with doing that to my brother."

"This does not concern you and your brother." Talbot lifted his arms out to his sides. Long talons slid free from his wrists.

Toby staggered back, terror a hot soup in his bloodstream. He'd been in a lot of battles in Afghanistan, and he'd faced and conquered many horrible fears, but this was beyond any fear he'd ever confronted. The mayor of Protection was one of Tagawa's childhood monsters.

Tagawa brought his sword overhead with both hands, shrieked something in Japanese, and lunged at Talbot.

The mayor jumped sideways and stabbed one talon straight into Tagawa's middle. Air leaked out of him with a kind of feral-cat hiss. Blood gushed from his mouth.

"Sho," Toby screamed.

Talbot lifted Tagawa into the air, skewered and dangling, and still holding his sword overhead. "You killed my son, and for that you will die."

Stink was frozen to the ground in absolute shock.

Toby jerked out his Alaskan and pointed it at Talbot with both hands. "Put him down, Mayor."

"You threaten me with a little gun?" Talbot's laugh was maniacal.

"This little gun will blow your fuckin' balls to Nebraska." Toby's hands were shaking. "Put him down."

Talbot flicked Tagawa off the talon. He flew through the air and slammed into the gutter in front of the only house across the street.

"As harmless as a water pistol," Talbot said to Toby. "I assure you." He grinned.

Toby had to call 911, get Sho some help before he bled out, but the mayor had to be put down first. "Get on the ground or I'll blow you away, Mayor or whoever...whatever you are."

Stink pushed himself up from the ground in front of the Roadmaster and wedged himself between Toby and Talbot. "Are you crazy?" Stink shouted at Toby. "You can't shoot him, for God's sake. Put the gun away."

Toby's eyes narrowed to slits, just the way Stink remembered them doing in Afghanistan during every bloodbath battle. "He's not human, Stink."

"You'll go to jail. Even if he's an animal, it's against the law to shoot him."

"Those weekend classes make you stupid, or what?"

"Your brother is right," Talbot said to Stink. "I am far from human."

Before Toby could even flinch, Talbot grabbed Stink from behind and pressed one talon point against his neck. The other talon was poised dangerously close to Stink's heart. "It makes no difference in the grand scheme of this world, or to me, but it might be better for both of you if Toby holsters that pistol before my wife shows up and there's more blood flowing in this street."

Toby's gun wobbled. "You get it now, Stink?"

Stink searched Toby's eyes for the answer as to how this tall, skinny mayor had such a powerful, tight grip across the front of Stink's chest. "Not sure I get much of anything right now."

Toby glanced across the road at Tagawa. The old man was still breathing in short gasps, blood spilling from his mouth, his fingers still tightly wrapped around the hilt of his Samurai sword.

"If we don't get help here soon, my friend ain't gonna make it, Mayor." Toby sighted his Alaskan, holding the heavy pistol at arm's length and pointed at the mayor's eye, the only clear shot Toby had. "Now back off before you make me do something you'll regret."

Talbot pressed his talon harder against Stink's neck, denting the skin. "Family is the most important thing in this world, Mister Gates. Would you agree?"

Toby remained silent, hoping he wouldn't have to pull the trigger and risk shooting Stink.

"Your Japanese friend killed my son."

"Your son was a monster."

"Granted, he was different than most kids..." Talbot was near tears. "...but he would have grown into a handsome boy. Your friend had no right to kill him. Evan never harmed anyone. Goddamn it, I found his head on the kitchen floor."

Toby saw fear in Stink's eyes. "How did we get in the middle of this shit, Toby?"

"Sho Tagawa warned me. I didn't believe him. Now I do. There are monsters in the shadows, and they live among us."

Tagawa hacked and shuddered then lay still. The sword fell from his grip.

Talbot shoved Stink aside. "It's over now, boys, go home."

"You killed him!" Toby squeezed the trigger.

The night exploded with a boom loud as cannon fire. A 454 Casull slug struck Talbot and blew his left arm off.

Stink took a direct hit from a shower of blood and bones.

Talbot just stared down at the ragged stump that once was his arm. "That's not possible."

"Then try this on for size." Toby fired four more shells.

Four more pieces of Mayor Talbot Lawrence splintered in a billowing red mist. What was left of him toppled over and hit the pavement with a decisive *splat*.

Porch lights winked on across the street.

Someone shouted, "Hey, I'm calling the police."

"Ah shit," Stink shouted. "How we gonna explain this to Sheriff Lockwood?"

Toby rushed to Tagawa and cradled his head in both hands. "I'm sorry I didn't believe you, old man."

Stink watched from a few feet away. "Is he dead?"

Toby gently set Tagawa's head back on the frost-covered blacktop. "Yeah." He thought about the money in Sho's coat pocket but couldn't bring himself to take it off the dead man. With a swipe of his palm, he closed the old man's eyes, like he'd done for many unlucky soldiers in Afghanistan. It didn't hurt any less that Sho wasn't a soldier. Toby removed his canvas field coat and placed it over Sho's face. "We'll get the other monsters for you, Sho. I promise."

"Toby? Have you thought this through?"

Toby stared at his brother. "There's more of these fuckers at the Darabont place. And we're going to kill them all."

Stink saw the anger in Toby's eyes, all right, but there was something else more profound. Duty. Toby had just found his place again, a soldier with a cause, a new war to fight. Afghanistan had come to Protection.

Toby reloaded the Alaskan. "Let's go."

"Stop and think, Toby."

"What's the matter? That Emma Naveed chick making you soft?"

Stink ignored the slight. "At some point we're gonna have to tell the sheriff what happened. We better at least get our story straight."

"There ain't but one story," Toby said. "The truth."

"Monsters? You think he's going to believe that? All he's gonna see is Mayor Talbot Lawrence lying in the street all shot to pieces. Overkill, Toby. You shot an unarmed man five times with a weapon that can bring down a grizzly with just one shot."

Toby glanced down at the late Talbot Lawrence. "Unarmed? You saw the talons come out of that freak."

"But where are they now? One arm's scattered all over the street in a million pieces. His other arm looks like yours and mine. Toby, we're in a heap of shit here."

"He killed Tagawa, and then he was gonna kill us."

"He told us to go home," Stink countered. "You lost your temper and blew him away."

"Whose side are you on?"

"It's the truth. Look—" Stink stopped.

Toby saw fear fester in his brother's eyes and

followed his gaze to Talbot on the ground. His legs were moving. "No way in hell."

Sirens wailed in the distance.

Toby and Stink backed up a few steps.

The mayor was struggling to get to his feet.

"Stink, looks like the mayor just solved our problem."

"What on God's green earth..?"

Talbot managed to stand, his knees quivering and ready to buckle. He looked down and took inventory of his injuries. His left arm was missing at the shoulder, his belly had three ragged holes straight through, and part of his right thigh was gone. He looked up at Stink and Toby, the expression on his blood-spattered face one of total surprise.

Toby held his breath as anger rose from the center of his chest. He squinted at the mayor, who was fighting to remain upright. The heat of rage pulsed up from Toby's neck and into his face. Pressure behind his eyeballs pounded harder.

Stink grabbed his arm. "Toby? What are we gonna do?"

"Remember that time in Ghanistan when Lieutenant Hanley bought it?"

"This isn't the time for reminiscing, Toby."

"Remember how we felt after we bagged the

body parts...and what we wanted to do to those lousy insurgents who killed him?"

Stink stared at his brother. "You're supposed to let it go, get on with your life."

"I'm starting to feel like that again."

"Toby, don't throw away six months of therapy."

"I see Jesse lying bloody at Doc Barnett's. I see Sho Tagawa bleeding out in the gutter."

"Toby...stop—"

"I'm trying, Stink. I truly am. But I can't push any of it out of my head...like I'm supposed to."

"I don't like it either, Toby. But this ain't Ghanistan, and this enemy don't die so easy. We gotta get out of here."

"We ain't going anywhere." Toby raised the Alaskan and fired point blank into Talbot's heart. His breastbone imploded, blowing his heart out through his back and shredding his spine. The body slapped the bloody street again.

"This is war."

Chapter 7

REID LOCKWOOD STOOD off to one side and watched Dr. Fitzgerald Collins, retired pediatrician who didn't appreciate being awakened in the middle of the night, put the toe tag on the second body lifted into the back of the EMT van. Protection and Comanche County were too small and too quiet to need a full-time medical examiner. Lockwood relied on Dr. Collins, who was beyond his seventieth birthday, to examine bodies when any strange circumstances were involved. The bodies tonight, with Mayor Talbot Lawrence being one of them, certainly fit that description.

Crime scene tape kept back the nosey neighbors, most wrapped in bathrobes and wearing slippers despite the cold. They murmured between themselves about hearing gunshots and loud angry voices.

It had taken over an hour for Collins and two

deputies, Hewey Black and Cole Hawkins, who Lockwood also had to wake in the middle of the night, to scour the street and nearby lawns for whatever remained of the late mayor. Body parts were strewn everywhere, and the deputies had already run through all their numbered place-markers and plastic bags. The body bag everything went into looked as lumpy as a sack of potatoes.

"I was looking forward to breakfast at Jennie's a bit later," Collins said to Lockwood. "No way can my stomach take any drippy eggs and greasy bacon now."

Lockwood, at a trim five-feet-ten-inches, leaned back against his county cruiser, a six-year-old Crown Vic, and watched Collins make notations on a clipboard. The makeshift M.E. was short, round, and always wore the same fedora and dark-gray suit. The latex gloves Collins wore did nothing to ward off the cold.

"What do you think?" Lockwood asked him.

He looked up from his clipboard. His old friend's eyes were bloodshot, and his breath vapors had frozen to his bushy gray mustache. Thick silver hair stuck out from under an official-looking sheriff's ball cap. "I think I'd rather be in bed dreaming about Grace Kelly. We'd be in Costa Rica where it's sunny and eighty degrees."

"Dr. Collins, I appreciate you being here...it's our mayor, after all."

"Was the mayor."

"I get your point," Lockwood said.

"What about them?" Collins gestured with his thumb over at Toby and Stink who were sitting on the curb, wrapped in old green army blankets and sipping coffee from Styrofoam cups. "The Gates boys did this?"

"So they say."

"I can pinpoint with one-hundred-percent accuracy what killed the mayor, one of those Alaskans in evidence bags on your car hood, but I'm not so sure about what killed the Asian gentleman."

Lockwood nodded. "Sho Tagawa."

"He was poked through by some kind of pointed instrument. Bled out in the gutter there."

"Maybe the sword?"

Collins shook his head. "It's coated with dried blood, but the metal is too thin and the wrong shape to have made the hole in Mister Tagawa's chest."

"So it can't be Tagawa's blood on the sword."

"There's another victim around here somewhere."

"And another murder weapon."

Collins shrugged. "We canvassed the whole area and didn't find anything else."

"That means there's a second crime scene."

"I do have another question, Sheriff. Why would those slow-witted Gates boys gun down the mayor? He seemed a decent enough guy."

"Don't know yet." Lockwood glanced over at Toby and Stink. They were both staring straight down into the gutter. "They're not talking."

"Have you told Lawrence's wife?"

"I called their place on Oak Street, but the housekeeper said the wife was in Bolivia. She thought the mayor was there, too. They've been going to South America on some kind of outreach every November for the last four years."

"I wouldn't want to be within fifty miles of the Gates boys when Mira Lawrence finds out they killed her husband."

"Meaning?"

"She's a knockout, no question, in that 1930's Hollywood style, but I firmly believe that woman could kill a man just by looking at him the wrong way."

"I don't know, Dr. Collins. What makes you say that?"

"I had one dance with her at that United Way

benefit last June. Felt like winter had snapped her fingers and rushed back in. I couldn't get warm for two days. I kept thinking..."

"What?"

Collins shook his head. "Nothing. Forget it. Probably just my imagination."

Lockwood wondered what the international area code was for Bolivia.

*****

Sheriff Reid Lockwood leaned back in his desk chair and glared at the Gates brothers. "I brought you here so we could talk without any interruptions."

From two ancient metal chairs on the other side of the desk, Toby and Stink looked at Sheriff Lockwood. "At least it's warmer in here," Stink said.

Lockwood remembered when Toby and Morgan Gates were the small terrors of the town twenty-five years ago. Stink Gates was never small, but even at ages seven, eight, and nine, those brothers caused so much hell that nearly every Friday or Saturday night a call came in to the police station, and Reid Lockwood, a rookie at the time, had to march down to the Gates' house for a little one-on-two conversation with the mischief-makers. Nobody else on duty wanted any part of that family, mostly because of Moss Hardy, the boys' stepfather.

Reid soon learned the other officers had figured Moss wrong, and if they had ever taken the time to get to know him, they would have understood how misunderstood Moss Hardy was, and mostly just because of the way he looked.

Moss spent his time splitting wood. The winter nights in Protection could get downright cold and miserable, and the only way to keep warm was with a wood stove sitting dead smack in the center of the house. With jobs in this part of the flatland being tight, Moss split wood for nearly the whole county. He would haul in the timber to his small place on the outskirts of town, and five days a week, everyone could hear the axe falling in four-second intervals, starting at sunup and ending right on the six o'clock dot.

Because Moss Hardy was a woodcutter, he had arms and shoulders like tree trunks. To say that he was not a man to mess with was like saying it got hot in Kansas during the dead dog days of August. He was actually a patient man and known for his even temperament. The same couldn't have been said for his stepsons.

"All right, boys. Tell me what happened."

"I told you we'd have to tell him," Stink said to

Toby.

"Shut up, Stink." To Lockwood Toby asked, "Do we need a lawyer?"

"I don't know." Lockwood leaned forward. "Did you do anything wrong?"

"Fucking right," Toby said. "I shot the shit outta the mayor."

Lockwood narrowed his eyes at Toby. "It's two in the morning, and it's just you fellas and me. I've known you boys for a long time, and I think we know what to expect from each other by now. You with me?"

The Gates brothers didn't say anything.

"I want one of you, and I don't care which, to tell me what happened."

"I'll tell you," Toby said. "But it may sound crazy."

Lockwood pushed his hand back through his thick silver hair. "Crazier than two men killed for reasons unknown in an otherwise quiet neighborhood on a cold November night?"

Toby proceeded. "Mayor Lawrence killed Mister Tagawa."

"You saw him do it?"

"He killed the Chinese man," Stink said. "I saw it too."

"Japanese," Toby shot back. "And *I'm* telling the story."

"So tell me..." Lockwood started writing notes on a legal pad. "How did Mayor Lawrence kill Mister Tagawa? We haven't found a murder weapon."

"Stuck him clear through his chest with...I don't know, some *bone* thing."

"Can you be more specific?"

"Never seen anything like it," Stink interjected.

Toby glowered at Stink for interrupting. "The mayor had a pointy bone that came through his skin, right out of his wrist."

"Some kind of fangs," Stink added. "But huge..." he swallowed, "and sharp."

"He stuck Tagawa with it and flung him to the gutter like a fish he'd just speared outta Kiowa Creek."

"You suggesting Mayor Lawrence was a monster or alien of some kind?" Lockwood's tone was incredulous.

"Just telling you what I saw."

"I saw it too," Stink added.

Lockwood jotted that down.

"I liked Sho Tagawa, Sheriff. He was brave. Had dreams of a peaceful retirement, gardening. And he cared about his family."

"I hear he bought the old Darabont place, right?"

"But it's infested with monsters. One of them damn near gouge out Jesse's liver. Tagawa killed another one."

"How?"

"Cut off his fucking head with a sword."

Lockwood wrote on the pad. "That accounts for the blood on the sword."

"Lawrence claimed the monster was his son."

Lockwood scowled at that.

"We're not lying to you," Stink said.

Toby shifted his weight and stared out Lockwood's office window at the glare of a streetlight. "I put five 454 slugs from my Alaskan into a fella who was skinny, barefoot, and wearing a bathrobe. His arm was blown clean off at the shoulder, part of his thigh was vaporized, and I could see porch lights through three holes the size of my fist in his middle. Ain't nothing on earth, Reid, and I mean *nothing*, can stay living after that kind of punishment." Toby leaned forward and braced his open palms on the top of his knees. "But no less than one minute later, before my gun barrel had a chance to cool, that skinny man started twitching, his legs started moving, and believe it or not, he got to his feet calm as could be."

Lockwood furrowed his brows. "Are you pullin' my leg, boy?"

"So I shot him again, right through the heart. I 'spect that put him down for good."

"Reid," Stink said, "can we go home? I got to work at the bank in the morning."

"Boys, let me ask you a question." Lockwood looked back and forth at Toby and Stink. "Was it self-defense?"

Toby took a breath. "I wasn't going to wait until he skewered me or Stink next to find out."

"So that's a yes?"

"Yes." Stink didn't say anything about Toby losing his temper and blowing six month's worth of PTSD therapy.

Lockwood eyed them both again then nodded. "Good enough for me. But if I didn't know you two boys for so many years, I might think otherwise. Lockwood took a long breath. "I can't be sure what the prosecutor might think when he gets here from Kansas City on Wednesday. Probably come down hard on me for not keeping you locked up. But, hell, for now, you're free to go home."

"We can't go home yet." Toby shouted. "We're going back to get the monster—"

"Sheriff took our guns, Toby."

"I'll be keeping them here for a while." Lockwood stood. "You boys stay away from that place. It's a crime scene."

Toby looked at the floor. "Then we gotta go out to the Prairie Motel."

"On 160?" Lockwood asked. "What for?"

"Tagawa's wife and daughter are holed up out there. Somebody's got to tell them the bad news. Feels like it should me."

"What are they doing way out there?"

"Scared off," Toby said. "Tagawa asked me to help him...with a rodent problem, I thought. Turned out to be mean-looking, hairy creatures that scared the women out of their own home."

"I'll check it out tomorrow," Lockwood assured them. "Meanwhile, don't give those women any details about what happened to Mister Tagawa until I'm done investigating."

Toby stood. "Be careful, Sheriff. I didn't hardly believe my own eyes, but when I was sure I wasn't seeing things, like having a nightmare or something, I had to rethink a lot I'd figured about monsters being myth and legend. They're real."

"I'll try to remember that."

Chapter 8

CONNIE ROOTS FINALLY settled down into the faded corduroy beanbag chair she had brought from her one–room apartment and stashed in the back corner of her favorite place to study in Protection. If she couldn't depend on peace and quiet in the basement of the new Comanche County Hospital Annex, the apocalypse was most certainly near.

She pulled a Snickers bar from the pocket of her blue hospital scrubs. Nursing student by day and orderly by night, she'd use her break times to keep up with her homework.

Things seldom moved down here, day or night. The only sounds she ever heard were the occasional dings of the elevator beyond the stainless doors and halfway down the hall.

This room was used for storage of old

equipment. And just down the hall, the morgue barely got three customers a year, so she pretty much had the place to herself.

Until now.

The elevator dinged and the steel doors banged open, bringing with it the sounds of squeaky gurney wheels.

She set down her textbook and half-eaten candy bar, cracked open the door an inch, and peeked out. Deputies dressed for the arctic wheeled two gurneys past her, each with a dark gray body bag astride. They clanged through the double doors and into the morgue. She closed the door to her hideaway and sat back on her haunches, wondering who had died. Two in one night...must've been a horrendous car wreck out on 160.

The deputies left, chattering, "Dr. Collins can take it from here," and "he can put them in the cooler," and "what a fuckin' mess," and "glad that's over with."

Their footsteps gone, she decided to investigate, see if she knew whose bodies were in the bags, and hoped that she didn't.

She slinked out of the storage room and padded toward the morgue. Her heart was beating so loud she feared someone would hear her. Once inside, her eyes were drawn to the gurneys, parked side-by-side, a scene of silent, motionless death. The only light came in from the hallway through two small windows in the double doors.

This first body bag did not take up the entire length of the gurney. The person inside had to be fairly short, a kid maybe, but hopefully not. Alongside the body, a bloody sword had been wrapped in plastic and tagged: *EVIDENCE.* She wondered if the sword was the murder weapon, but who got killed by swords these days? The tag on the body bag read: *Sho Tagawa.* The name didn't ring a bell so she moved to the other gurney where the body bag looked lumpy. The tag on that body read *Talbot Lawrence.* Now that name rang a bell.

The mayor of Protection was dead.

Her stomach lurched. She thought she would be sick right there, but the elevator chime stopped her gag reflex. Dr. Collins could show up at any moment. If so, she'd have been busted for sure.

She rushed to the door, peeked out, and heard footsteps receding down the hall in the opposite direction. Her mouth turned dry with fright and then relief. She knew right then she should run back to her hideout, put her nose back in her textbook, and forget about Lawrence and Tagawa...but she didn't.

Swallowing her fear, she returned to the mayor's body bag and gripped the metal zipper. Her fingers trembled so badly she could hardly pull it down. When she did, a retched stench hit her in the face, the smell of blood, and bowel, and death.

She looked for the face of Mayor Lawrence within the black opening of the bag. There was familiar white hair, clumped and bloody, and the face was wrenched in such a painful grimace that it was unrecognizable. The sight was so horrid she couldn't look away. Her heart was beating in her throat like a trapped rabbit.

A faint rustling came from nearby. She turned her head to see the foot of the body bag moving. Her eyes widened, and the rabbit started screaming in her throat.

She stumbled backward in disbelief that two feet were kicking inside the bag, a desperate attempt to get out. Someone had made a horrific mistake. Probably that old guy Dr. Collins. He'd bagged a live body...a body that was now sitting up and reaching for her with one blood-soaked hand.

Chapter 9

STINK THOUGHT IT WAS a terrible idea to truck on out to the Prairie Motel at this time of the morning and wake what was left of the Tagawa family with incredibly bad news. But Toby had insisted, and once his brother got an idea stuck in his head, it was impossible to get it unstuck. One look at Toby sitting rigid and upright in the Roadmaster front passenger seat told Stink his brother was on a mission of his own.

He slowed the Buick as it approached the old motel's gravel parking lot. The Prairie Motel had seen better days but was clean and well maintained by Closet Dixon and his son LaVertis, who had played running back on the Protection High Jack-Rabbits football team, back when Stink was a sophomore. Closet had played running back himself, back in the late sixties before he enlisted, did two tours in Nam,

and received a bucket full of shrapnel, much of which was still lodged inside his right hip.

Stink rolled the big sedan past the Prairie Motel sign with the deep green neon letters and into the parking area. A black man in his mid-sixties waved to the Roadmaster from the motel's office window.

"Closet must never sleep." Stink stopped the car near the motel office. "I'll ask him which room —"

"No need." Toby pointed through the windshield. "Only one room with the lights on. They're waiting up for Sho."

"You sure?"

"I would be if my daddy was late."

Stink nodded.

They stepped onto the gravel. The motel office door swung open, and Closet Dixon gimped outside. He was medium height and build and wore a well-worn canvas field coat. A half-smoked but unlighted Camel drooped from between his lips. "Boys. What brings you out here?"

"Hello, Mister Dixon." Stink rounded the front fender.

"Too damn cold to be running 'round this time of night."

"We're sorry." Toby joined Stink in the cold. "Can't be helped."

"How's Cassandra doing?"

Toby took an icy breath. "As good as can be expected."

Closet nodded. "Be sure to give your momma my best."

"We will."

"And Moss?" Closet asked. "That stepdad of yours doing all right without the missus?"

Toby looked at the lighted window. "Moss ain't been the same for a while... Look, we gotta talk to Tagawa's wife."

Stink said, "Bad news."

"About that Japanese fella?"

"Will you excuse us?" Toby started toward the room with the bright window.

"What the hell's going on, boys?"

"Won't be but a minute," Stink said and caught up with Toby.

Closet yelled, "Tell LaVertis to get his ass back here and go to bed."

The brothers welcomed the heat inside Tagawa's motel room. His wife, Haya, was apparently prone to being chilled, so she had the furnace cranked up as if a glacier was parked next door.

LaVertis, Closet's son, had answered the door. "What are you fellas doin' here?"

"Ma'am," Toby said to the woman in the wheelchair, her face expectant and full of hope. Her gray hair was wrapped up in a bun with a shiny black stick poking through it, and she wore a black and gold kimono patterned in birds and leaves. A grandma-knitted blanket lay across her lap. Kasumi sat on the bed, her tired eyes fixed on the strangers at the door. She was a surprise to behold, maybe twenty-three years old, rail thin in a pink miniskirt and white blouse. Her straight blond hair wasn't the surprising part. It was her skin, black as LaVertis's and smooth as sunshine.

"I'm sorry to come here like t-this," Toby started, but...

Stink jumped in. "Bad news, we're afraid."

Haya's expectant face tightened, every line a fissure fixing to crack wide open. "Where is my husband?"

LaVertis closed the door and rushed to Kasumi's side, reaching her as she got to her feet. "Father. Where is Father?"

Toby dipped his chin. "There's been an accident."

Stink slugged Toby's shoulder. "No accident. He was murdered."

Haya screamed. "Oh, no, no, no, please..."

Kasumi fell to her knees at the wheelchair, grabbing for Haya's flailing hands. "Mom. Mom. Oh, Mom."

Toby elbowed Stink. "You have as much finesse as a train wreck."

"Well, you said it was an accident. That ain't right."

Haya cried, "What happened to my Sho?"

"He's gone, ma'am, that's all we can say."

The two women wept and groped each other in a way far too familiar to Toby and Stink. Too many times they'd seen the same gut-wrenching reaction from Afghan women who'd lost a loved one to war, insurgent attacks, or Taliban shootings. The shock and sorrow of death were universal.

LaVertis excused himself to the porch. Toby signaled Stink to follow him. "Let the women grieve in private."

Now they welcomed the cold, and the three men stood together and avoided the heartache with small talk.

"Haven't seen you down at the firehouse," Stink said to LaVertis. "Guys say they miss taking your poker money."

LaVertis was five-foot nine, two-hundred-thirty-five pounds, and would be a load to tackle once he picked up a head of steam. "I surely don't miss losing to them. Last month I almost couldn't make the payment on my Trans Am."

The former high school football star's prized possession was a 1972 Pontiac Trans Am, glistening black with the trademark firebird decal on the hood. He often said if Darth Vader drove a car, this would be the one.

Stink slapped him on the back. "Who sold you a car on time payments?"

LaVertis squared his shoulders. "My pappa. Used to be his wheels. Sat in our garage for more than thirty years, waiting for him to decide I was ready to pay for it. Total true value, nothing should ever be just handed out."

"Sounds like Closet was planning ahead."

"I got her runnin' real good, too."

The motel room door opened, throwing a wedge of light on the ground followed by Haya's mournful sobs. Kasumi stepped out. "Now," she said to Toby with her back to her mother. "Tell me exactly what happened."

Toby blinked. "Already told you all I can."

Kasumi took one step closer to Toby. She looked him straight in the eye. "That tells me nothing."

"You should hear the details from the

sheriff...tomorrow maybe."

She put her hands on her hips. "It already is tomorrow."

"Your daddy was very brave." Stink's eyes flicked to her knees and back up.

"Shut up, Stink," Toby said. "Your mouth has already done enough damage."

"She has a right to know."

"Let the sheriff tell her, after his investigation."

"Somebody better spill it," Kasumi shouted. "And I mean right now."

Stink said, "It wasn't pretty—"

"I said shut up, bro."

"Was it something in that dreadful house that killed him?"

Toby took a deep breath. "All right. I'll tell you, Kasumi. But you're not going to like what you hear."

She closed the door on her mother's sobbing and waited in the cold, seemingly unaffected.

"It wasn't one of them creatures, not directly."

"Then who murdered my father?"

"More like *what* killed him."

"You're talking in circles."

"Whatever it was, it looked like the mayor of Protection."

"Why would the mayor kill my father?"

"That's where it gets complicated," Stink said.

LaVertis chimed in. "What's he talking about?"

Toby held up a hand. "All right, I'll just say it." He paused for a breath and then let the words come out. "Sho killed one of those creatures, and the mayor claimed it was his son, and he killed your dad with a sharp bone thing that came out of his wrist. So there, that's it in a nutshell."

Kasumi stared out across the mostly deserted parking lot. Her jaw muscles were flexing like crazy. Then she pushed open the motel room door, stepped across the room, and picked up her sword from the corner. She gripped the hilt with the intricate brocade and rested the flat edge of the blade in her other hand. Then she returned outside, stopped within one foot of Toby and glared at him with hard eyes. "You expect me to believe that bullshit?"

Toby flinched and backed up a step. "You'd have believed it if I was the sheriff tellin' you."

"You should've let Lockwood tell ya," Stink put in.

LaVertis said, "Hey, Kasumi, take it easy."

"Believe me, I am taking it easy." She flashed the sword in Toby's face. "Who the fuck are you anyway?"

Toby stared at her, not backing down. "Your

father hired me tonight—"

"And me," Stink added.

"Hired you for what?"

Toby shoved his freezing hands into his pockets. This was going to take a while. "He showed me everything, told me about the noises at your place, and what you guys caught in those traps. The monkey arm, whatever it was..."

Kasumi's eyes lost focus. She inched back and leaned against the wall. "I saw it too. My father must've had a great deal of faith in you."

"I didn't believe him at first, but then I saw one for myself, and another one attacked my dog."

"So...how does the mayor fit in?"

"I guess your dad was in shock or something, found him wandering the streets. We were headed back to kill the grunt that damn near killed my dog when the mayor showed up outta nowhere, standing barefoot in the middle of the street. Your dad knew he was bad news, got out of the car to kill him."

"We tried to stop him," Stink said.

"That's when the mayor told us the grunt was his son."

"He was major-league pissed," Stink said.

"You mean to tell me you two men couldn't handle one old, barefoot mayor before he killed my father?"

"The monster in him took us by surprise."

"Fuck." Kasumi hung her head. "Now I've got to go kill the mayor. It will honor our ancestors."

"Beat you to it," Stink said.

She looked up, mouth agape.

"Toby blew a hole in his heart."

"It was him or us," Toby said.

"If the mayor is the monster you say, then I don't believe he's dead."

"Come on, get in the car. We'll show you."

Chapter 10

MIRA LAWRENCE PACED the front foyer of the old Darabont Mansion. The entire first floor was coated in a fine film of dust. Nothing remained of the residents who had lived here before: no furniture covered with sheets, no boxes or trash, no drapes or blinds to cover the dirty windows. The walls were devoid of decorations, picture frames, and sconces; not even the hooks were left behind. The place was as barren and bleak as her heart felt. She worried a path back and forth. Talbot had been gone far too long.

At the entryway window, she stopped and looked out, hoping to see him on his way back from wherever he'd run off to. Her eyes scanned the vast, empty darkness. There were no signs of life at four in the morning. This entire town was dead, winter and summer. There were no art galleries, dance clubs, fine dining, or IMAX theaters. Nothing ever happened here. Protection could have been so much more for her, her family, and her kind. Instead, it remained a town of shadows and secrecy.

She hated this place.

If it was up to her, that would change. But it wasn't up to her. She had hoped Talbot, as mayor, would bring new life, new businesses, and new hope to Protection, but he didn't, not that he couldn't; he wouldn't...

Her son, Ephram, waddled up beside her. She reached down and scratched the back of his neck. He'd lost an arm, and now he'd lost his brother. A forlorn whimper escaped his throat.

Dread built up inside her like a wall of fire. Her firstborn son was missing. The last she'd heard of Evan was the screeching of a frightened little boy. Then nothing. Talbot had gone looking for him, and now he was missing.

She should have gone with him. She could have helped him find Evan. Talbot was a good husband, completely devoted to his family, and he had never given her a reason to worry.

But now she knew something was wrong...terribly wrong.

Movement at the end of the street.

Her eyes flicked. She moved closer to the

window. A figure was limping, staggering, toward the house. He was wearing blue and bloody hospital scrubs.

Her breath caught in her throat. *Talbot.*

She pulled open the front door and rushed outside.

Chapter 11

DR. FITZGERALD COLLINS BROKE every hospital rule there was about not smoking and lit a Swisher Sweet cigar. The body on the concrete floor at his feet was truly one for the books. He'd come to the morgue to put Lawrence and Tagawa on ice and discovered what was left of Connie Roots, nursing student at KSU and resident of Russell where her parents lived. Blood type AB negative, and she was an organ donor.

Not that she's likely to be donating any organs now.

The elevator down the hall dinged. Collins turned, took his Swisher from his lips, and exhaled a puff of smoke. The stainless double doors swung open. Sheriff Lockwood, the Gates brothers, and an African-American woman walked into the morgue.

Lockwood studied Collins, who looked even more rumpled than he was a couple hours ago. "Just got the call."

"I see you brought the Brothers Grimm along."

"I ran into them out front."

Collins shifted his gaze to Kasumi. "She shouldn't be in here."

"She's with us," Stink said.

"What's with the sword?"

"Mister Tagawa was her father." Lockwood gestured with one thumb at the gurney with the sword and body bag on top.

"Oh. Sorry for your loss, Miss," Collins said. "But you should go back upstairs."

"She wants to see her father and his killer," Toby said in her defense.

"I'm a little busy right now." He puffed on his cigar.

Lockwood stepped closer to Collins and stared down at the covered body on the floor. "Who is it this time?"

"Connie Roots, nursing student. The girl took study breaks in the equipment room down here. I stumbled on her when I came in to put our homicide victims in the cooler."

Lockwood bent to the floor and lifted the covering. The naked body appeared flattened, the limbs skin and bone, the head collapsed like a shriveled up prune under a tangle of hair. "What the hell happened to her?"

Collins shrugged. "I've never seen anything like it."

Lockwood stood and faced Collins. "Give me your best guess."

"I've seen it before." Toby stepped up. "The girl had everything inside her drained out."

Collins agreed. "Most all of the body liquids have been sucked out along with her internal organs."

"Like a spider does," Stink said. "It injects digestive juices into an insect and sucks everything dry."

Lockwood turned to Toby. "Where have you seen this before?"

"At the Darabont Mansion."

"He's right," Kasumi said, "because that's what was happening to mice and rats that were caught in the traps. And I saw the monster that did it."

"Me too," Toby said. "I told you so, Sheriff."

"My father hired Mister Gates to help him get rid of those horrible monsters."

"And me," Stink said.

Lockwood let that settle.

Kasumi walked to the gurney with the body bag and sword. "This must be my father."

Collins nodded.

"Mind telling me how he was...killed?"

"Stabbed. He bled to death."

"Stabbed with what?"

No one said anything.

She pointed at Toby and Stink. "These two geniuses told me they shot the mayor, said he had a sharp bone that came out of his wrist. Is that true?"

"They told me the same thing," Lockwood said. "But they weren't supposed to say anything to you about the mayor."

"He's dead, right?"

"Unfortunately."

"I want to see the body."

Lockwood nodded and looked around the room. "Would that be all right with you, Dr. Collins?"

"If I said no, would that stop you?" Collins stepped to the far gurney and discovered the body bag was smeared with blood, as was the zipper, and the bag seemed flatter than it was earlier. He looked around the room with panic in his eyes. "Something's not right here."

Lockwood rushed up. "What is it?"

"The body is gone...like the mayor got out of a sleeping bag and zipped it back up."

"How did he get out?" Kasumi asked.

Both men looked to the body on the floor.

"She must've let him out," Collins said.

"And the mayor killed her," Lockwood added. "What the hell for?"

"He fed on her," Stink said. "Like the spider—"

"Shut up, Stink."

Kasumi ran out of the morgue.

Chapter 12

TALBOT LAWRENCE LAY on his bed, stared at the plaster ceiling, and thought how the spreading cracks looked like tiny Louisiana river deltas. Some of the best times of his life were ages ago in the humidity of Baton Rouge, its lush vegetation, and living with people rich in Cajun culture. Nothing like Protection, Kansas: flat, treeless, dusty...

He thought about being born and named Tamir Lapinski and how he changed his name many years later, so that he might better blend in with the different societies where he lived. He'd chosen the name *Talbot Lawrence* after watching the movie *The Wolfman* that showed at one of those drive-ins in Wichita where he'd moved with his immigrant family.

Those old black-and-white horror films didn't scare him. He knew the real horrors of the world were a thousand times more frightening than mythical werewolves and vampires. In fact, he felt empathy for those creatures that were either born to their fate or were dragged into something terrible due to no choice of their own. Just as his lot in life had turned out for him, born to this fate and forced into this life of obscurity.

Life seemed much brighter, though, after he met Mira Goldstein. He remembered that rainy day, the smell of wet asphalt in the school parking lot, the tall slender form of a girl gliding toward the building like a ghost from a fairytale. She wore a gray coat, a deep blue skirt that stopped just above her knees, white ankle socks and saddle shoes. Her dark hair glinted with random streaks of deep red. She was the most beautiful sight he had ever seen in Wichita. She'd thrown him a quick smile, and at that very instant he was certain his heart was no longer his own. She had captured it without speaking a word.

At this moment, it wasn't hard to remember why he'd moved to Protection, Kansas. For protection. Nothing ever happened here. He could hide in plain sight.

But Mira had other plans. She hated living in the shadows. She'd convinced him to run for mayor so he could make a difference in Protection, put some life in this dead town. However, he resisted drawing attention to her, their family's secret, and their clan. And now, he was suffering the consequences of not keeping a low profile. The Japanese man had forced him to defend himself, the Gates brother had retaliated, and now the entire town would know Talbot and Mira were not really one of them.

He needed to rest, but no matter how he tried, he could not drift back to sleep. He had been so weak just hours ago, so close to complete darkness, but now images kept pushing at his temples. The young girl, so foolish she was to unzip the body bag. He had sprung up and drained her through his one remaining wrist fang until every ounce of life within her became his. As he fed, she deflated and flattened in his clutching arm. No thought had gone into killing her, just instant reflex. He did not feel a trace of guilt, though the recent memory pressed the image of that girl's face into his mind, and he wanted to forget her look of abject horror.

Maybe if he could reach to his nightstand and switch on his cassette player, the soothing sixties music would help rid his mind of her face. However, with his left arm only a regenerating stub, he wouldn't be able to push the play button while he held himself up with his good hand.

For some reason, the pain in his shoulder had faded, while the stinging ache in his hip had steadily increased. He managed to sit up about an hour ago, but the effort had created shockwaves of pain that tore up his right side. He'd endured the pain to stagger home, but now any effort to stand, much less walk, wasn't worth the agony.

He would have to wait a couple more hours and try again.

The pain must have been truly distracting, because he didn't notice the tall, black woman until he saw her at the foot of his bed. She held a mirror-finished sword in one hand at her side, pointed at the floor.

"Are you Mayor Lawrence?" the woman asked.

With his good hand, he pulled the sheet up to his neck. "You surprised me. How did you get into my house?"

"The basement door was open."

"I must've forgotten to close it." Talbot studied his uninvited guest. The woman was lean and muscular, and her face was creased with anger. Normally he wasn't afraid of anyone, but now... "Who are you?"

"Kasumi Tagawa."

Talbot stared at her. "Miss Tagawa, I'm not in

very good shape to entertain guests—"

"So you don't recognize my name?"

"Should I?"

Kasumi tightened her lips. "You killed my father."

He blinked. "I don't recall killing any black men."

"Japanese. I was adopted."

"Ah, the Japanese man. What makes you think I killed him?"

"Don't play riddles with me. I was at the morgue."

"So was I. Frightful place."

"Obviously you weren't dead."

"And you're here to rectify that, I suppose."

"You catch on real fast, Mayor."

He studied the young woman. "Would it be inappropriate to ask a favor of you first?"

Kasumi stared at him, mute.

"My cassette player. I cannot reach the buttons."

She squinted. "What's a cassette player?"

"Right there. On the table. Just push the play button, if you don't mind."

"Why should I do you any favors?"

"There's a song I'd like you to hear."

"I came here to kill you, not listen to music."

"Then I will be dead in a minute, what's the harm?"

"No tricks."

"I promise."

Kasumi moved to the nightstand, located the play button and pushed it.

Music filled the air. *A long, long, time ago...*

Talbot said, "This song is so sad."

"What of it?"

"It's about the day the music died."

"What's that got to do with anything?"

"Nothing is more sad, Miss Tagawa, than the premature death of a child. You agree?"

She shrugged, having never given it any thought.

"A father should never have to experience the death of his son. Nature did not intend that to be the order of things."

"If you say so."

"Your father killed my child, my son. Cut off his head with a sword. And yes, I killed your father for doing that."

Kasumi gripped the sword with both hands and raised it over her head. "My father was the most quiet, gentle man ever born to this earth."

"Before you strike me dead, there is something you should know."

"What?"

"Allow me to show you." The bed sheet descended from his chin as Talbot shifted his legs to the edge of the bed.

The cloying smell of decayed flowers struck her.

He grimaced, touched his bare feet to the floor, and straightened, only to wobble as he faced her upraised sword.

The man wore a bloody t-shirt. An incredibly short arm and stubby hand, as though he was born with a terrible deformity, barely poked out from the left sleeve. A gnarly hunk of meat that once was his thigh drooped from his skivvies.

Her stomach compressed and a shiver raced up her backbone. "What happened to you?"

"Gunshot wounds, biggest I've ever seen. Blew out my insides, blew out my heart, shattered my spine...oh yeah...I was dead in that morgue. Dead as your father lying next to me with his sword. And now I'm alive, so you should know that your sword cannot kill me."

"If I cut off your head with it, you will die, just like your son."

His face paled with fear. "Please...when I awoke yesterday morning, I did not set out to cause your father any harm, Miss Tagawa. My son did not set out to hurt anyone either. We are peaceful living in the shadows. It was your father who brought death to our door."

"He was protecting his family."

"As I was protecting mine." He sat on the bed, head slumped, chin to his chest. "We both failed miserably." He sobbed. "So do what you must do." Talbot closed his eyes.

She inhaled. The Samurai sword sliced through the air with barely a sound.

Chapter 13

TOBY'S RADIO ALARM blasted Steppenwolf's *Born to be Wild* at 7:45am. After only two hours sleep, Monday morning was hell on earth. Stink had to be at the bank in fifteen minutes, but Toby found him crashed on the couch, his camo jacket on the floor and his boots still on his feet. Toby lifted the quilt Stink had pulled over his head. "Stink, wake up." Toby shook his brother's shoulder. He was out cold, snoring away, and in no shape to go to work and guard anyone's money. Toby decided to fill in for him.

Last night on the way home, they'd killed precious sleep-time on a wild goose chase looking for Kasumi at the Darabont Mansion. She wasn't there and she wasn't at the motel either. LaVertis was looking after Haya until Kasumi returned. By then Toby was too tired to care where she'd gone.

Protection

He opened his front door. Frigid air slapped him in the face. He'd normally drive five blocks to the bank, especially in bad weather, but the battery in his jeep was dead, and he wasn't about to go fishing through Stink's pockets for the keys to the Roadmaster.

So he walked. He shoved his hands into the pockets of his parka and missed the familiar presence of the Alaskan. Since that gun was missing in action, he'd strapped on a shoulder holster and his Kimber .380, which could pack a pretty good punch in an emergency, not that any emergency at the bank had ever happened.

Toby used his key in the terribly old-fashioned lock of the bank's front entrance, pulled open the glass door, and stepped inside. He pushed buttons on a wall-mounted keypad to disable the night alarm, locked the door behind him, and started the morning routine of lights, turning up the heat, nudging the copiers and printers into action, and most importantly, making his first cup of coffee.

Working security in the Bank of Protection on Broadway had to be the easiest job in town. He basically just exchanged hellos with customers all day. The job was so completely boring, he'd sit on a stool near the front door and read gun magazines.

The chance of bank robbers bursting in was about as great as Protection, Kansas, instantly becoming the water-skiing capital of the nation.

A teller, Maggie, came in through the back entrance and readied her cash drawer for the morning rush, which usually consisted of nobody showing up before ten o'clock. Frank Rinaldi, the assistant manager, stood at his desk on the edge of the lobby, shuffling papers. Frank's eyes were sunken, and his hair uncharacteristically pointed straight up in several spots. He looked as though he may have had a worse weekend than Toby, if that were possible. Rinaldi nodded as Toby walked toward the door.

"Morning, Frank." Toby stopped at the front door and glanced back at the wall-mounted clock above the three teller stations. He sipped coffee, set his mug on a countertop, and unlocked the door.

Gazing out at the morning traffic, he chuckled as he watched the few cars that passed by on Broadway. He retrieved his coffee and took another sip. The sad part about the whole thing was that one or two cars passing by was as busy as the street would get all day. Downtown Protection could hardly be described as *bustling*.

His eyes focused on a woman across the street, walking toward the bank. He managed to swallow his coffee and take one step back from the door.

***

Stink's eyes popped open. A quilt covered his face, so he pulled it off while his brain scrambled to make sense of his position on the couch. Why was he sleeping in the living room? He rubbed his eyes with the back of one hand and glanced at the quilt over his body. He didn't remember anything about how that quilt got there. And he was still wearing his boots.

He found his feet and staggered through the house looking for Toby. Then Stink realized he was late for work. "Shit." It quickly became apparent that Toby had gone in to the bank to cover for Stink's shift. Again, he was looking out for his younger brother just like Toby always did since they were kids.

Stink remembered the town bully, Lenny Lingrosso. After he dropped out of ninth grade, he'd set about perfecting his life's work as a hulking, uneducated ruffian. He hung out most afternoons on the sidewalk that led from school, waiting for any poor sap to attempt to pass by him without paying the Lenny toll. Stink hated him with a deep, unrelenting passion, and even though Stink had grown to nearly Lenny's size, he always paid the toll rather than get into a fistfight with him.

Stink had nothing to fear. He was starting right offensive tackle on the school football team, but being Lenny's favorite and perpetual victim became an embarrassment, especially when Lenny's bullying intensified to ransacking his backpack and threatening to beat his face in, even after he'd paid the toll.

He'd never told anybody about Lenny Lingrosso. As far as his parents knew, Stink would toss a football with some of the kids on his way home, and that was the reason for his dirty face and soiled clothing after school. Much more than the embarrassment, Stink was truly afraid if his stepdad found out how Lenny Lingrosso was pummeling him, Moss Hardy would march on over to the Lingrosso's double-wide trailer on the far edge of town, take Lenny with one hand by his shirt, and tell him to stop bothering Stink Gates.

The embarrassment alone would have killed Stink, having his stepdad fight his battles for him. So Stink said nothing and endured the torture and humiliation.

Being two years ahead of him in school, Toby had a different schedule, and usually left the building about twenty minutes after Stink, so even though the two of them made the morning trip together, they never walked home at the same time.

One afternoon, Toby didn't feel good and asked the nurse if he could go home early. Permission granted, he joined up with Stink to walk the half-mile trek home.

Sure enough, Lenny was on duty harassing the younger kids on their walks home. He was not intimidated by Toby, or anyone else, so when Lenny saw Stink and Toby casually walking toward his sidewalk turf, the first thing he thought of was how his considerable reputation would be enhanced after he beat up Toby Gates.

Before Toby and Stink got within fifty feet of him, Lenny blocked the sidewalk, hands on his hips, shoulders back, and chest puffed out.

The story about what happened next was never told. Stink and Toby never talked about what happened to Lenny Lingrosse's face, how his nose got broken and both eyes turned black and blue, and Lenny never told his parents or called the cops, or ever showed up on the sidewalk again. But to this day Stink never forgot how Toby had taken care of business for his younger brother.

Stink sank into the sofa and let his mind regroup from only three hours of sleep. He couldn't let his brother bail him out today. Even though nothing ever happened at the bank, it was his job to be bored all day. He spotted his camo jacket on the floor, snatched it, and stumbled out the front door to his Roadmaster.

***

Toby watched the woman approach the bank. She was attractive in an Alfred Hitchcock film heroine sort of way. She was olive skinned. Her hair was a deep brown with reddish streaks, and she looked trim and athletic with round shoulders and shapely legs. She wore a sleeveless gray dress and impractical heels but no topcoat of any kind, even though the temp outside was in the mid-twenties.

She reached the bank door and peered inside. Toby stared at her face from the other side of the glass, fascinated at the beauty. Her shimmering blue eyes could've cast a spell on him. She pulled the door open and stepped in.

"Excuse me, are you Mister Gates?"

"Yes." Toby inhaled the scent of dried flowers, like moldy potpourri. "One of them."

She studied him. Her sleek arms hung at her sides. She clenched and unclenched her hands.

Toby stared. "Pretty cold morning for no coat."

"I'm cold every second of every minute of every day."

"Maybe if you dressed warmer."

She smiled. "Or maybe if I moved to a warmer place than Protection."

"Gets downright sweltering in the summer."

She took a long breath and let it out. "My husband is a good man, Mister Gates."

"I'm sure he is." He didn't have a clue who her husband was, and he struggled to remember why this woman looked familiar.

She blinked. "Is there a place we could sit?"

"Are you here to attend to some banking business..." he glanced around for any sign of a threat, "or are you some kind of distraction?"

She waved a manicured hand across her face. "You flatter me, Mister Gates."

"Didn't mean to, ma'am. What do you want?"

"A place to sit, remember? We need to talk."

Frank Rinaldi appeared beside her. His necktie was pushed only part way up and twisted off-center. He guided his arms into the sleeves of his topcoat. "You may sit at my desk, miss... er... missus?"

"How nice of you, sir."

"I'm off to get some triple extra dark espresso. Be right back." Rinaldi scurried out the front door.

Toby offered the woman a chair in front of Rinaldi's desk and leaned on the edge. "Okay, talk."

"How does one judge a good husband?"

"Maybe I ain't the best person to ask. Have you tried Ann Landers?"

She crossed her legs and placed her hands on one knee. The scent of dead flowers again filled the air. "Kindness," she said. "Kindness."

Toby shrugged. "So you know the answer to your own question. Good for you. I'm not a marriage counselor."

"He is kind to me, Toby, his wife of many, many years, even when I am cruel to him. He is a gentle poet, and he's devoted to his children, year after year, season after season."

"Sounds like a good guy. Why should I care?"

Her lips edged back in a half smile. "Talbot's kindness is what sets him apart."

Toby narrowed his eyes at her. "So you are Mrs. Lawrence."

She closed her eyes. "Do you know, Toby, where my husband is right now?"

Toby's brain rushed back a few hours to the empty body bag on the gurney. His heartbeat started hammering. "Matter of fact, I don't know where your husband is."

Her eyes popped open, wide and mean. "He is at home."

"That's odd."

"Home recuperating."

Toby tried to make sense of what the woman was saying, but his head felt like mush, and he suddenly regretted taking Stink's shift at the bank this morning. "I hate to be blunt, Mrs. Lawrence, but your husband should be dead. And now he's AWOL from the morgue."

Mira ran her chalk-white fingers of one hand back along the side of her face. "Talbot told me you shot him last night."

"I gotta be honest with you, ma'am. I did shoot him. I shot him a lot. In fact, I don't mean to be insensitive, but I blew his fucking heart into the next county."

"How could you do that to him?"

"How could he not be dead?"

She gazed down at her hands, now gripped tightly together in her lap. "Talbot has always been a fast healer. I expect he'll be back to his old self by this time tomorrow."

A shiver attacked the back of Toby's neck. Tagawa's monsters wouldn't go down easy, if ever.

"Now, Toby, may I ask you a question?"

"Sure."

"Why did you shoot my husband?" Mira's blue eyes darkened.

He swallowed. "Your husband murdered my friend."

"The Japanese man?" She glowered. "He killed our son."

"Your so-called son attacked him."

"Evan would never hurt anyone. He was just a boy."

Frank Rinaldi pulled open the front door and stepped over to his desk, toting a huge paper coffee cup in one hand. His cheeks were bright red from the cold. "How you folks doing?"

Toby stood. "The lady was just leaving."

Mira looked up at Frank, and then back at Toby. "I suppose it doesn't matter."

"What doesn't matter?" Rinaldi lifted the coffee cup to his lips and sipped loudly.

She looked at him. "Toby, is this man your friend?"

"Friendly enough, I guess."

"As I was saying, Mister Rinaldi, I suppose it doesn't matter why Toby shot my husband last night."

Frank swallowed the coffee and blinked. "I-I think I left my phone at Jennie's. You two take your time. I'll be right back."

Mira stood before he could take one step and

blocked his escape. "My child's death is something with which I have yet to come to terms. Tagawa has already paid the ultimate price for killing an innocent child."

Toby stood upright. "That creature didn't look like an innocent child to me."

"The fact remains, Toby, you assaulted my beloved husband. That is something a good wife cannot tolerate." A long sharp bone slipped out of Mira's right wrist.

Toby reached for the .380 Kimber under his coat.

She twisted to the side, jammed the pointed bone straight into Rinaldi's thigh, and before the man could flinch, she pulled it back out in one fluid motion. Blood jettisoned from the wound. Rinaldi staggered, held his coffee in front of him as if he was afraid to spill it on his way to the floor, screaming.

Toby jerked out the Kimber. "Get on the ground, lady."

Mira laughed in his face. "You can't possibly think that little pea shooter can hurt me?" Her back was to the door, and the morning glare coming in from the street surrounded her until she was mostly a blurred silhouette.

"Frank did nothing to you, lady."

"You attacked my husband, and now I have

attacked your friend. Fucking simple as that."

"Are you shittin' me?"

"This is only the beginning, Mister Gates." She turned and strutted out the door.

Chapter 14

STINK PARKED THE Roadmaster on the side-street by the bank. Before he could open the car door, a woman in a gray, sleeveless dress came out of the bank and casually strolled by. Stink thought somebody might be filming a TV commercial, which would actually have been a first for Protection, Kansas. He could think of no other good reason for this babe with movie star looks to be waltzing down the street with bare arms in sub-freezing temps. Stink sat and watched her until she disappeared around the corner. Then he remembered he was late for work.

A siren sounded from nearby. Stink pushed open the car door and stepped into the frigid air. Two police cars swerved to a quick stop on the street in front of the bank. An ambulance screamed up and parked beside the police cars. Stink sprinted for the bank's front door.

***

Dr. Fitzgerald Collins knew when his third call to rush to a crime scene in less than twenty-four hours came in, he probably should start thinking of full retirement, sooner rather than later. But at least this time, the body he was to examine turned out not to be dead.

The EMTs bustled about Frank Rinaldi, assistant manager of the Bank of Protection. The mid-thirties man had a severe puncture wound completely through his right thigh, and if it were not for Toby Gates, who applied immediate battlefield medical treatment, Frank Rinaldi would have bled out and died long before Dr. Collins and the EMTs had arrived on the scene.

Collins watched as Rinaldi was wheeled out on a gurney, just as Reid Lockwood and two deputies walked through the front door. Lockwood looked as though he hadn't slept in a month.

"You look terrible," Collins said.

Lockwood glanced over at Toby Gates, who was in a chair, wiping blood from his hands with a red-stained towel. "What the hell happened?"

"Let Toby Gates fill you in. I'm driving to Tucson, Reid."

"Tucson?"

"My daughter and her husband live there with Faith, my six-year-old granddaughter, who still thinks visiting with grandpa is a cool thing."

Lockwood just stared at him.

"Protection is supposed to be a quiet town, Reid, far off the beaten track and famous for its slow-paced, rural living. It is not supposed to be the basis for the next TV sci-fi crime drama."

"What the hell? You can't just walk out on this town. We need you. I need you."

"Watch me." Collins shuffled out the door.

"Prick." On his way toward Toby, Lockwood dodged his deputies as they strung their yellow police tape. "What the hell, man?" He pointed to the blood streaks on the floor.

"Mrs. Lawrence stabbed him in his leg," Toby said. "Took me off guard."

"She's in Boliva."

"Tell that to Frank." Toby threw down the bloody towel.

Stink rushed in. "What happened to Frank? They hauled him off in an ambulance."

"She has one of them bone things too."

"Who?" Stink asked.

"The babe in the gray dress is the mayor's wife.

Mira Goldstein Lawrence."

Stink grumped. "Damn. I missed all the excitement."

Lockwood lowered himself into the chair beside Toby. "Did you shoot her?"

Toby pulled the Kimber pistol. "Wouldn't have done no good." He placed the gun on Rinaldi's desk. "Check for yourself, it hasn't been fired."

Lockwood picked up the small pistol and sniffed the barrel. "At least that's one report I won't have to write."

"But I wanted to shoot her. I most surely did."

Chapter 15

REID LOCKWOOD STEPPED from his cruiser and took a moment to study the house on East Pine. It was a modest ranch house with well-tended shrubs and a concrete walkway so clean not even one stray leaf, twig, or unruly blade of grass dared touch its immaculate surface. A tall, wire-fenced dog-run jutted out from the side of the house.

Lockwood walked to the front door and knocked. He waited. About twenty seconds later, Lockwood knocked again. He waited.

The door opened. An elderly man looked at Lockwood. "Reid. Good morning," the man said with a Polish accent. He had thinning silver hair and matching mustache, and he wore a thick sweater.

A pit bull appeared, sat beside the old man, and stared up at Lockwood with huge yellow eyes. Her light gray hair was streaked with pink.

"Good girl, Lilly," the old man said. "It's the sheriff who's come to visit."

Lilly whined.

Lockwood scratched the top of her head with his fingertips. "I've always enjoyed her company on poker nights. She likes me whether I'm winning or losing."

Her eyes scrunched shut as he scratched her massive, boxy head.

"Ben, you took a while to answer the door. I hope I'm not disturbing you."

Ben Guralnick shook his head. "When men with guns knock at my door, I am careful about answering."

"Funny man." Lockwood tapped snow from his boot toe against the threshold step. "Are we going to stand out here in the cold gawking at each other?"

"Come on inside. Hot tea or coffee?

"Coffee sounds good."

Ben moved aside as Lockwood took the one step up and into the foyer. The old man closed and locked the door behind them, and then walked to the kitchen with Lilly at his side.

Lockwood followed.

Ben strode to his coffee maker on the kitchen counter. "Long night?"

Lockwood sat on a chair and rested his elbows on a small tabletop. "Odd night."

Coffee poured, Guralnick set two steaming mugs on the table. He pulled a chair back and sat across from Lockwood. "Odd how?"

Reid pursed his lips and glanced around the room. "I need your help with a case."

"What do you got, Reid? A missing dog?" He chuckled into his mug then took a sip.

"Ben, I know you don't think much of the paranormal stuff—"

"No such thing."

"No ghosts, goblins, or UFOs in your world?"

"Things are either normal or abnormal. Paranormal is meaningless."

"How about supernatural?"

"Could be, say a woman lifting a car off her child. That's supernatural and believable."

Lockwood blew steam off his coffee. "When you helped us with that case last year—"

"The joint task force in Wichita?"

"Yeah, that one. We thought the paranormal might be at work. You set us straight, though. Nothing paranormal. Just one normal, everyday psychotic killer."

"Glad I could help. Whatcha got now?"

"I think this one will change your mind about paranormal."

The old man stared at Lockwood. "I doubt it."

Lockwood forced a smile. "You have a sixth sense for solving mysteries." He took a sip of hot coffee.

Guralnick cleared his throat. "Go ahead. Humor me."

"Mind if we go for a short ride? I got something to show you."

Guralnick gazed into his coffee. "Shame to let this go cold for nothing."

"When you see this, you'll need something much stronger."

Ben placed the mug on the table. "I'll get my coat."

***

With Lilly seated in the front between them, the old man stared straight ahead through the police cruiser windshield as if in deep thought, while Lockwood guided the Crown Vic along the side streets. Lockwood could think of nothing to say, so he decided not to say anything until he stopped the car. They'd have plenty to talk about real soon.

Lockwood wondered what was going through

the man's brain and if he was able to push aside any preconceived notions and open his mind to something new, something horrifying, something unexplainable. He seemed both fragile and strong at the same time, and that contradiction never failed to confuse the hell out of Lockwood.

The winter sun sparkled off the front windows of the Darabont mansion as he stopped the Crown Vic at the deserted curbside. "We're here."

"Spooky old house. I debunk these things for breakfast."

"Prepare for a full-course meal." Lockwood opened his door.

Ben eased his old frame out of the big sedan, tucked his hands in the pockets of his topcoat, and gazed at the pathway that led to the front entrance.

Lilly followed and settled beside him. She pressed the side of her head against his leg.

Lockwood stopped beside them on the cracked concrete of the sidewalk. "This appears to be the center of some weird shit." He looked around. "It's been empty for years. We come around to check for broken windows, kids partying inside, despite the rumors of how old man Darabont disappeared ages ago. Here one day and gone the next."

Old Ben said nothing. His eyes were fixed on the

crumbled stone steps of the front porch.

"About three, four months ago—"

"There is a difference, Reid, a distinct difference."

Lockwood blinked. "What are you talking about?"

Ben looked at the ground and turned back toward the police cruiser. "I'm cold."

"What the fuck is the matter with you?" Lockwood stared at the old man. "I want to take you inside the house."

Lilly whined. Her back quivered. Her eyes were fixed on the house.

Ben reached for the car door handle. "I'll be more comfortable in your office, if it's all the same to you."

Lockwood grumped, "Sure, Ben. Sure."

"Lilly, come."

The dog hopped up into the front seat.

Lockwood and Guralnick dropped inside the car. Lilly draped her front paws across Ben's legs. Lockwood started the engine. Ben kept his eyes shut as if he'd seen enough of the Darabont Mansion.

***

Mira stood inside the front door of the mansion and peeked out through the dirty glass. She had spent the last few hours holding her beloved husband as close as she could. The sound of a vehicle arriving outside had pulled her out of the basement, and she had bounded upstairs to investigate.

Outside, the sheriff's car was parked at the curb. An old man and his grey dog stood rigid as stone gargoyles planted on the sidewalk and stared at the house with permanent, fixed gazes. A flicker of long-discarded recognition pushed at the back of Mira's memory, a photo she'd seen, a warning she'd heard, a man to be wary of.

The sheriff accompanying the old man didn't help settle her trepidation. He'd been here earlier with his deputies, searching the house. They'd all left scratching their heads. Now this. She'd have to retreat to the basement, gather Ephram and Talbot together in a locked room, and hide in complete silence again. This was no way to live.

She was about to sound the alarm when the old man abruptly turned back to the car. A brief argument followed; she couldn't hear their words, just read their body language. Then the dog jumped into the car, the men got in, and the car sped off.

It appeared something had frightened the old man.

She shook off her worry and rushed back toward

their basement residence. She needed a long, scalding shower, and a change of clothes. Then maybe she would be able to consider her life in this wretched place with a clearer head, a life that had just led to one of her children being executed. She had yet to deal with that worst of realities, the loss of a child. She had not even seen Evan's body. Talbot had hidden the remains and cleaned up the blood to save her the anguish and spare the world from her wrath. But she would soon find him and prepare a proper burial.

And then there would be hell to pay.

Chapter 16

JESSE SKITTERED ACROSS the shiny wood floor and jumped into Toby's arms as if the little dog knew freedom was only moments away.

Toby rocked backward from the force of the dog's jump. "Whoa, boy."

"Jesse looks in good shape and spirits," Stink said.

Toby held Jesse close as the dog licked Toby's jaw. "Guess he's happy to see me."

Doc Barnett jotted in Jesse's medical file. "He didn't try to bite or lick at the wound. And the stitched area is healing faster than I expected. No infection. But I'm giving you a cone to take with you in case the guy changes his mind when you get home. Stitches can get to itching sometimes."

"Thanks, Doc." Toby hugged Jesse. "I mean it."

Doc coughed and wiped his nose with a tissue.

"I've got to say, Jesse is one smart canine. The way he studied me when I checked on him, I thought he was about to speak to me."

"He'd tell you thanks if he could, I'm sure."

"How's Cassandra's cat doing?"

"Mister Jumpers is just fine, Doc."

Stink reached over and scratched Jesse's head. "Who loves ya, boy? Good boy."

"Anyways, Doc, we're in your debt."

Doc nodded. "Bring him back right away if there's a problem."

Toby carried Jesse to the door, pushed it open with his foot, and stepped outside.

Stink extended one massive hand to the doc. "What Toby said."

Doc Barnett handed Stink the doggie cone. "Take good care of that mutt."

***

Ben Guralnick sat in an uncomfortable chair beside Lockwood's desk and cradled a mug of hot tea with both hands, trying to absorb the heat from the ceramic.

"Want to take off your coat?" Lockwood perched on the edge of his chair and shuffled through some papers.

"I prefer to keep my coat on. Seems I've been allergic to the cold for a long time."

"It can get brutally frigid out there."

Ben settled back and took a breath. "There is still time to change your mind about this case and walk away."

"I don't walk away from anything. What's on your mind?"

"If I tell you what's happening at that old place, long-forgotten history will be revealed."

"History?"

Ben swallowed. "And in the end, you'll be sorry. We'll all be sorry."

"Quit talking in metaphors, Ben." Lockwood leaned back in his chair. "Get to the point. What spooked you at that old house?"

"There has been an odd death in Protection, yes?"

"How did you know? We've kept it under wraps."

Ben tapped his index finger against one gray temple. "The pictures inside your head. I see Mayor Lawrence, don't I?"

Lockwood's jaw dropped. "Jesus. Do you mean to tell me that you can read minds?"

"Not exactly. I get visions."

"Like a psychic?"

"Images only. Not thoughts. You've seen studies where psychics guess what card a subject is looking at?"

"Yes."

"They get it right, say half the time."

"The results vary, I guess."

"I don't guess. That's how I solved your last case."

Lockwood shrugged. "I-I don't know what to say."

Guralnick placed one hand flat on the desk. "Now let's talk about why you've come to me for help."

"Okay."

"Are you a fan of time-travel stories?"

Lockwood thought about it. "Like The Time Machine? Sure."

Guralnick set his mug on Lockwood's desk and pulled his topcoat collar closer to his neck. "If we were to time-travel back to, say, the Middle Ages and take with us an object as simple as a flashlight, the people there would surely believe something supernatural was at work."

"Probably scare the shit out of them."

"There is nothing supernatural about a flashlight.

It was created by scientific design, not hocus pocus or Wicca mumbo jumbo. And there is nothing evil about a flashlight."

"Of course not."

"There is a distinct difference when comparing the normal, or the abnormal and supernatural to something that is pure evil and created for the express purpose of propagating that evil. Do you understand the difference?"

"I'm not sure. Explain it to me."

"When I was seven years old, I witnessed pure evil created by evil."

Lockwood frowned.

"I was confined to a concentration camp in Poland and put to work in a laboratory for Major Walchok, a Nazi scientist."

"I don't get the connection."

"Let me tell you the story."

"Okay."

"For sixteen months I served as Walchok's assistant. I lived in a spotless laboratory residence, showered, dressed in clean clothes, and was fed modest meals."

"Ben, what does all this have to do with what's going on around here?"

"Patience, Sheriff. I'll get to it. Serious men in

long gray coats came into the laboratory. They brought with them prisoners of all ages and sizes, cleaned up and dressed in plain white smocks. The men injected these poor people with a dark blue liquid...straight into their necks."

"Like they were lab rats?"

"Sometimes they sat up, apparently unaffected, but most times they went into convulsions and choked to death on their own vomit. Those who survived were called *Walchoks*. They had very unusual and dangerous powers of strength and speed, and they were hard if not impossible to kill. The Nazi's constructed special containment cells to keep them in. Horrible conditions..."

"What was the point of these Walchoks?"

"I was a kid. How was I supposed to know? But now I understand...the Nazis were developing super-humans to help them win the war. But the Walchoks were useless because they were not controllable."

Lockwood slowly sat up in his chair. "So you're saying these monsters in Protection are the Walchoks?"

"I could smell them at the Darabont house. Dead dried flowers. I'll never forget that smell."

"So that's why you wanted to get out of there so fast."

"When the allies advanced into Poland, the Nazis abandoned the camps, but before they fled, they let the Walchoks loose."

"And some of them made it here, to Protection."

"A great place to hide. Nothing ever happens here."

"Why are you here? Seems kind of coincidental to me."

"When I came to America, I made it my life's ambition to track the Walchoks by investigating abnormal events. My journey to Protection began with the unexplained death of a high school girl in Kansas City. No witnesses, which seemed odd, as the death had occurred in the shower room after gym class."

"Kansas City is a long way from here, Ben."

"Strangely, right after the death, one student moved away quite suddenly. Her name was Mira Goldstein, and I traced her parents' records back to Poland and the very camp where I was imprisoned."

"Both her parents?"

"They escaped Europe together. Now that I had a name, I tracked her to a Wichita high school where she met Talbot Lawrence."

"If you suspected her for the death of that girl in Kansas City, why didn't you contact the police?"

"Do you believe any of this I'm telling you?"

"Not really."

"Then why would they believe me?"

"Point taken."

"Mira and Talbot eventually married, but she got into trouble again, damn near exposed an entire clan with a hair brained plan to open a cultural arts center. She and Lawrence were banished. I lost their trail until I learned that Talbot Lawrence had become mayor of Protection."

"So you moved here."

"I was hoping to find the entire clan."

The chair squeaked under Lockwood's shifting weight. "If you knew the Walchoks were here, why did the Darabont house spook you?"

Ben leaned forward. His eyes focused on Lockwood. "It's where they breed."

The sheriff felt a knot twist in the center of his chest as the undeniable facts began to flood his brain. Walchoks had been living among the good folks of Protection, in the shadows or in plain view, like the mayor. And it was his job to root them out, which at this moment seemed an impossible task.

Chapter 17

MIRA FELT THE AIR COOL OFF a few degrees as she found her way back down the basement stairs. She reached her living quarters and stopped when she saw Talbot sitting upright and motionless on the edge of his bed. "You shouldn't try to get up yet."

"I'm fine."

She glanced around the room. "Where's Ephram?"

"He's getting tall, you know."

"Talbot—"

"So fast." He gazed up at her and smiled. "I forget how quickly our children grow. It shouldn't surprise me, but it always does."

She knelt by the bedside, took both his hands, and cradled them in her own. Tears pooled in her eyes. "What's wrong?"

He took a long breath. "She had a sword, Mira,

just like her father's."

"Who?"

"And with one swing, she could have cut off my head."

Mira felt the blood rise in her face. "Please lie back down, Talbot."

"She could have ended my life, Mira." He stared at her. "My beloved Mira...but she didn't."

She released his hands and stood. "Tell me about the woman with the sword."

Talbot leaned back against the pillow. His eyes caught movement behind Mira. "Ephram."

Mira turned. Her son stood near the door, about four feet tall, human arms and legs almost fully formed. New skin showed where large clumps of hair had shed, his chin and one cheek now smooth and radiant. A couple of his baby teeth had fallen out. By tomorrow he'd have his new adult teeth. Already, a blue hue began to glow from his irises. "Come over here, son."

Ephram wobbled to his mother, wrapped his gangly arms around her middle, and pressed his head against her stomach.

She hugged her son. "Talbot? We've always spoken plainly to each other."

"Yes."

"So listen to me now." She waited until his eyes met hers. "I do not blame you for Joshua's death."

He blinked. Joshua, another dead son before Evan.

"In all these years, we have lost one of our children only once before. And we got through it, as hard as it was."

"There's no getting through it, no getting over it. I miss him every day."

"I too wake some mornings after dreaming about Joshua and wonder what he might be like today."

"Mira, I'm sorry. I shouldn't have let him go outside and play."

"And now Evan is gone, too, because you let him run loose in the house." She took a breath. "But how could you have known the dangers so close to home?"

Talbot gazed at his wife and felt his stomach twist. He hated seeing her upset about anything, and he hated the fact he was responsible for her sadness even more.

"We cannot let this happen again."

Talbot clenched his jaw. "Of course not."

"The people of Protection have killed two of our children." She pressed her hand against Ephram's back. "I will not allow it to happen to this child, or to any others we have in future seasons."

"What do you suggest? We move. Run again? How—"

"Leave that to me." She released Ephram and sat on the mattress, leaned to Talbot and kissed him gently on his forehead. "First, we will move to the attic of the main house."

"What? No, Mira. I like it down here."

"The basement is not safe any longer. The swordswoman found you. So can others. You'll move up there now while I find the woman and kill her."

"No, Mira. She had her chance to finish me off but didn't and walked away." He showed her the gash in the pillow where the sword had struck instead of his neck. "She's no threat."

"Everyone in Protection is a threat." Mira's eyes narrowed. "I want you to rest up there with Ephram. Promise me you will stay hidden until I return."

"Return?" Talbot swallowed. The look on his wife's face was unsettling. "Where are you going?"

"Wichita."

Talbot's eyes got big around. "It's too dangerous to go back there."

She fluffed his pillow. "I'll be careful."

"What are you going to do?"

"Start I war, I hope." Mira took a breath. "We'll

never lose another child ever again."

"Please, Mira, there's been enough killing."

"That is for me to decide, not you." She gave him a wan smile and stepped out of the room.

Chapter 18

CASSANDRA GATES STARED UP at Henry as the pudgy, middle-aged caregiver placed a flowered dish of tuna noodle casserole on the TV tray beside her wheelchair. She felt as if she deserved no more attention than a hound dog at feeding time. Henry had his eyes fixed on the TV screen.

Sally Field was crying. So was Jessica Lange.

"I've seen this movie about four hundred times." Henry put one foot on an ottoman and rested his hands on one knee. "Best movie ever."

"I wasn't watching it."

Cassandra rarely watched TV, even though she kept the small flat-screen turned on nearly all the time. The noise comforted her, made her feel as if she was still part of the outside world.

"You okay, Mrs. Gates?"

"I'm not hungry."

Henry cleaned his hands with a disinfectant wipe. "Don't blame you one little bit. I have to eat this slop, too. Reminds me of what they fed us at summer YMCA camp. Only thing missing is the grape Kool-Aid. Bug juice, we called it."

She gave him half a smile. Henry wasn't that bad, as compared to her string of caregivers during the past six months. He was always positive and took the time to actually speak with her. That was more than she could say for most.

Henry said something about the movie, but Cassandra tuned out his voice and gazed at the photos on the small table beside her chair, as she did every night, a kind of ritual that kept her family close to her, and real. She and Moss were smiling and had their arms around each other as blue-toned mountains stood regally in the background. That trip to Utah was the last one they had taken together before the accident. She focused on a larger photo of her boys, Toby and Morgan. They were much younger, before they went to war, standing beside a huge elk they had just downed in the woods of Colorado. A smaller photo showed Jesse, her loyal black-and-white mutt, posing in the grass beside her cat, Mister Jumpers. That photo, more than the others, for some reason, sent a terrible, hollow rush right to the pit of her stomach. How she missed those critters. She began to weep.

Henry rushed up behind her. "Mrs. Gates, what's wrong?"

"I'm so unhappy here."

"But your rehab is going so well."

"Henry." She sniffled. "I'd like to skip physical therapy tomorrow morning, if it is all the same to you."

Henry did not answer. The scent of potpourri wafted through the air. She turned her head. A woman with striking features, auburn hair, and the palest of skin, stood behind her. "Hello, Cassandra." Her voice was like syrup, though overly smooth and sweet.

"Who are you?"

The woman chuckled. "I once was Mira Goldstein, but now I go by Mrs. Talbot Lawrence. You may call me Mira."

Cassandra felt a shiver at the base of her spine. Why had the mayor's wife come to see her? She glanced around the room. "Where's Henry?"

"Your friend will be fine. Let's just say he's taking a nap." She pointed to the floor behind Cassandra's wheelchair.

Henry was stretched out on his stomach across a

throw rug. His lips formed a half-smile, and he seemed to be peacefully asleep.

Cassandra's heartbeat jumped. "What did you do to him?"

"Family is the most important thing in life." The over-elegant woman looked out the window at the restful expanse of Evergreen Gardens' front lawns. "In fact, family may be the *only* important thing."

"What do you want?"

"I want to know if you agree."

"Of course, I agree."

"Good. Then we have some common ground."

"Get out or I'll call security." She searched for her remote call button, but it had been moved out of her reach.

"I'll be leaving soon enough." The pale-skinned woman gripped a cushioned chair across the room, and with one hand easily lifted it and moved it to face the wheelchair. She sat and crossed her legs. "So hear me out."

"Why should I?"

"Because I'm in charge here now." Her voice dripped venom.

Cassandra wrung her hands in her lap. "Please don't hurt me."

"Who is this gentleman?" Mira pointed to one of

the photos.

"Moss. Moss Hardy."

"Your husband?"

"I married him when my boys were small."

"And their father?"

"Wyatt Gates. He passed away some time ago."

Mira nodded. "Was your husband a good father?"

"My boys grew to think of Moss as their dad."

"Sons need a strong father."

Cassandra swallowed. "Is this about Toby and Morgan?"

"Your sons, yes."

"What did they do this time?"

Mira squinted at her. "May I ask you a personal question?"

"No."

"What happened to your legs?"

"Tell me what my boys did that brought you here."

Her eyes narrowed. "I want to know about your legs. Then we'll talk about your boys."

"All right. Car accident. I'm paralyzed from the waist down. Moss was injured, too. He lost a leg."

"That's too bad."

"I'm in rehab here, learning how to take care of

myself enough to go home to Moss and my boys. They need me."

"A family needs their matriarch."

Cassandra's hands trembled. "Please...what about my boys?"

Mira stood and pushed up her blouse sleeve, exposing the flawless white skin of her forearms. "They don't deserve you."

Black fangs slowly extended from her wrists.

Chapter 19

STINK TOOK HIS BOWL of Grape-Nuts with milk from the microwave and stepped back into the den. Toby was still sitting in the cracked leather of his favorite chair, and Jesse was curled on his lap, eyes closed.

Toby had not said a word since they left the vet clinic. Now he sat motionless in that chair, like he was snake-bit and paralyzed with his eyes wide open.

Stink settled on the sofa, ate a spoonful of warm Grape-Nuts, and studied Jesse. It was good to have the little dog in the house again. Stink hadn't realized before how empty the place was without him trotting around on the wood floors, his nails clicking and clacking on his way from window to window, inspecting the perimeter as a good watchdog should. Right now, Jesse was in a pain-pill dead sleep.

Two raps sounded from the front door. Stink

looked at Toby. Neither he nor Jesse moved. "I'll get it," Stink muttered, set his cereal bowl on the coffee table and stood. He glanced out the front window to the porch and saw Kasumi standing there in a black leather jacket and short pink skirt. Her knees were shaking. "What does she want?"

He opened the door. Cold air rushed in.

"Mister Gates. May I come in?"

Stink regarded the scabbard slung over the tall woman's shoulder. "Sure." He stepped aside.

"Thanks." She moved past him and entered the front hall then padded into the den where she stopped when she saw Toby and Jesse. "Toby, are you all right?"

He did not answer.

Jesse raised his head a few inches and squinted at her then lowered his chin back across Toby's knee.

"I apologize for disturbing you," she said to Stink.

"No problem. How 'bout some warm Grape-Nuts? I was going to make a proper dinner, but Grape-Nuts suddenly sounded good."

She shook her head.

"Let's sit, then." Stink gestured at the sofa.

Kasumi eased down on the edge of the battered denim slipcover. Her skirt hiked high up her ebony thighs but she kept her knees together. "Is your brother all right?"

"He's had a lot to deal with. Jesse getting hurt hit him pretty hard."

"Is your dog okay?"

"He's healing fast." Stink turned his back to Toby and lowered his voice. "They have been real close since our momma rescued the pooch from a shelter in Topeka about four years ago. Sometimes I think Jesse is the only living thing Toby talks to about private stuff."

"I'm glad he's okay."

"Where have you been?"

"I was walking all night and lost track of the time. I was damn cold, too."

"Short skirt and that little jacket ain't no way to dress for a cold night. Your momma okay?"

"I hope so, since I haven't been back to the motel and haven't spoken to LaVertis either."

"Can I get you some coffee, something hot?"

She shook her head.

The sofa creaked as he sat on the other end of the denim slipcover. "What's on your mind?"

Kasumi stared at the throw rug on the floor. "My father... My father taught me more than swordsmanship."

"I'm sorry he's gone."

"He taught me honor, confidence, and bravery." Kasumi sighed. "I was just an orphan kid when I was given the best gift ever, a family."

"My stepdad, Moss, he was big on family, honor and bravery, doing the right thing."

"Has he passed on?"

"Nah. My real dad died when I was little." Stink glanced at the floor. "Moss still lives in our old place...where Toby and I grew up. He keeps mostly to himself these days, 'cept when he goes to Wichita."

"What's there?"

"Our momma is in rehab. She's paralyzed."

Kasumi nodded. "Take it from me, spend as much time as you can with him, and with your mother, both you and your brother, while you still have the time."

"We do what we can."

Kasumi gazed down at her hands. "Don't dishonor them as I have dishonored my father."

"Don't see how that could be true."

She didn't say anything.

Stink decided to not ask any more questions and wait until Sho Tagawa's daughter was ready to let him know what she was doing in his living room, and why she was talking about her dead father.

Kasumi took her scabbard from around her shoulder and placed it across her lap. She sniffled then took a crumpled tissue from a jacket pocket and dabbed at her eyes. "I went looking for the mayor last night."

"We know. Tried to go after you. Couldn't find you."

"I found him."

"Where?"

"Back at the Darabont house. He was in bed, recuperating, talking to me about his cassette player."

"He had a cassette player? I got one in my Roadmaster."

"His arm was growing back. He had terrible wounds that were heeling. I had my sword."

Stink stared at her.

"But I couldn't kill him. My father did not train me to be an assassin."

"Training is different than real combat, no question. But how could you kill him when Toby couldn't?"

"Cut off his head, that'd kill him. It would have been honorable to avenge my father's murder. Honorable. Can you understand that? I swung my sword, but struck his pillow instead. I am a coward."

"Don't say that."

Toby cleared his throat from across the room. "Stink."

Jesse opened his eyes and squinted up at Toby.

Stink had forgotten his brother was still in the room. "Were we talkin' too loud?"

Toby cradled Jesse in his arms and got out of the big leather chair. "Meeting. In the kitchen."

"But—"

"Now."

"Sure." Stink looked at Kasumi. "Want me to get you something while I'm up?"

She shook her head.

"We'll be right back."

***

Toby crowded Stink against the kitchen counter. "Ever notice when there's a babe involved, your brain starts working in slow motion?" He shifted Jesse in his arms. "A cassette player? Are you kidding me?"

Stink stared at his brother. "I have no idea what you're talking about."

Toby shook his head. "She tells you a dead man was talking like nothing's happened after I shot him full of holes, and his cassette player seems odd to you?"

"We're not dealing with normal here."

"There comes a time when we just gotta let things go, Stink. We don't need to get any more involved. Tagawa's dead. The mayor's body is missing. Let Reid sort through it."

"You're not getting any argument from me." Stink said. "Jesse pulled through just fine, but what about the grunt that hacked him up? You still going back to kill the little fucker?"

"No. I'm gonna let that go, in case the thing is just a kid like the mayor was saying."

"That's not like you, Toby. Maybe them PTSD therapy sessions been working for you."

"Too bad your linguistic classes haven't helped you one bit, brother."

"No argument again."

"I feel damn bad for Tagawa's daughter. In another life, Kasumi might have been the little sister we never had."

Stink groaned. "In another universe, you mean."

"Yeah. She' got us both outclassed."

Someone rapped on the front door.

"Now what?"

Kasumi stuck her head in through the kitchen doorway. "Sheriff Lockwood is here."

Toby and Stink groaned.

She retreated back to the front room. The

brothers glanced at each other then followed her.

Reid Lockwood stood motionless with his hands shoved in his jacket pockets just inside the front door as if he was afraid to take another step inside. "Boys."

"Come to arrest us, Reid?" Stink said.

"What for?" Kasumi asked.

"Long story." Toby didn't like the edgy look on the sheriff's face. "What is it now?"

The room was nearly silent except for a pop or two from the fire in the wood stove.

Toby, Stink, and Kasumi exchanged confused glances.

Lockwood shifted his weight. "I got a call from the sheriff in Wichita at about 6:30."

Toby felt his throat tighten. A call from Wichita couldn't be a good thing...

"W-Wichita?" Stink stammered. "This about our momma?"

"You boys should get your coats."

Stink squinted at him. "What happened?"

"I'll drive," Lockwood said.

Chapter 20

KASUMI STUDIED THE ELDERLY gentleman who wore the overcoat and fedora, riding next to her in the police cruiser. The old man stared out the back seat window and watched the endless winter cornfields, all gray and flat, fly by. She wondered why he'd come along on the trip with them in the first place.

On the ride to Wichita, she sat between the old man, Ben Guralnick, as the sheriff had introduced him earlier, and Toby Gates, whose face had turned three shades of purple with worry. Jesse rode on his lap and stared out the window the entire journey, as though he was mesmerized by speed and motion or on the lookout for a lost four-legged relative. Stink hadn't said much of anything from the front seat. The Crown Vic could have been a rolling hearse, as quiet as everyone was.

Protection

Once parked at Evergreen Gardens, they all scrambled into the assisted living center together, Toby and Stink in the lead. "Where is she? Where is our momma?"

Kasumi held back behind the sheriff and his companion. For an old man, his gait was strong and purposeful.

Wichita police officers milled about, comparing notes. "Stabbed clear through the stomach." "Something long like a sword." "But round like a spear."

And an emergency medical team attended to a man on a gurney, asking him if he knew what day it was and who was President of the United States. He kept saying, "A beautiful woman...a beautiful woman."

Staffers herded curious old folks down the hall. "The excitement is over. Everyone back to your rooms."

The local sheriff stepped up to Lockwood. "She had a visitor, a woman. Staff says she was over-the-top elegant. Walked in without saying a word, walked out without saying a word. Smelled moldy, too."

"Mira," Toby growled out.

"Where's our momma?" Stink demanded.

The sheriff ushered Toby, with Jesse in his arms, and Stink into a room. Through the open door, Kasumi saw a drawn curtain in front of a bed, and someone had parked a wheelchair off to the side.

Within seconds, the halls echoed with wails of grief and curses of anger. Toby stormed out of the room and collapsed on the floor, hugging Jesse and muttering about monsters.

Stink kicked the wheelchair and fell to his knees.

Kasumi retreated to the lobby where the air smelled of potpourri and Pledge. She stood near a fake plant with white flowers and fought back tears of her own.

The old man, Mister Guralnick, stagger-stepped up to the reception counter, leaned on his elbows and buried his face in his cupped hands.

She edged up beside him. "Are you all right, mister?"

He turned to her, his eyes tight with fear and one word on his lips that she didn't recognize.

"Walchoks."

***

If the ride to Wichita was the hearse, then the ride back was the closed coffin. It was near midnight before they arrived in Protection. Tires crunching gravel, the Crown Vic pulled into the lot behind City Hall. The small building was nestled against the Post Office and housed one courtroom and offices for the Protection Police Department and the Comanche County Sheriff.

Kasumi stepped out of the car and into a blast of winter air. She followed the men who marched silently to the door. The only sounds inside were the static coming from a nearby police scanner and their own footsteps on the scuffed tile floor. She stopped at a desk and picked up a phone without asking anybody for permission.

A young deputy pulling the graveyard shift nodded at them as Sheriff Lockwood led the group into a small conference room. On a countertop sat a half-full coffee pot. "Help yourself." Lockwood poured old coffee into a mug while the others found chairs or suitable places to stand. Toby held Jesse and petted his head. Nobody said anything.

Kasumi stepped in. "Sorry, I had to call the motel to check on my mother."

"How is she?" Toby asked.

"She can't sleep. LaVertis is with her. His dad is on his way here."

Lockwood looked up from his mug. "Closet is coming here?"

"I told him what happened to Cassandra. He said he wanted to help us get those fucking Walchoks."

"How do you know about Walchoks?"

"I heard Ben say the word. He said it three times. Walchoks. Doesn't take genius to know what he meant. I think he owes us all an explanation."

Toby gritted his teeth and leaned back against a wall, Jesse still in his arms. "What is she talking about?"

Jesse licked Toby's clenched jaw.

Guralnick got antsy in his chair.

Lockwood said, "Ben, time you tell the others what you told me."

Guralnick cleared his throat and addressed Toby. "It wasn't your fault."

Toby raised his eyes. "Scuze me?"

"For what happened today. In Wichita. You couldn't have known."

"How could I?"

"I sense you feel guilty, perhaps because you could have done something to prevent what happened."

"You're right. I should have shot Mira when I had the chance. How did you know?"

Lockwood jumped in. "Ben has...a special

psychic talent."

"Yes. I see things, feel things—"

"Bullshit," Stink said.

Guralnick smiled at him. "Tell me about the young lady with the green eyes."

Stink paled. "I...ah...Emma?"

"She is quite pretty. A teacher, right? English?"

"Linguistics. How did you know?"

"Go on, Ben," Lockwood said. "They deserve to know the whole story."

Guralnick closed his eyes, told them about his time in the camp, the Walchoks, and then he opened his eyes. "After a time I realized Walchoks had a distinct aroma."

"Aroma?" Kasumi said.

"Like dried flowers," Toby said.

Ben acknowledged that. "I smelled that fragrance the instant we walked into Evergreen Gardens."

Toby squeezed his eyes shut and slid down against the wall to the floor. He held Jesse tightly to his chest as if the small dog were his last friend on earth. "You're telling us Momma was killed by a monster created by a Nazi mad scientist?"

"Mira is the offspring of two of them. A genetic freak created by evil for evil purposes."

"Somehow I've got to tell Moss about

Momma...how the hell am I gonna do that?"

Stink had a bigger question. "How the hell did these Walchok monsters get here from Poland?"

"After the war, many Europeans fled the destruction and poverty and emigrated to the U.S. Here, they blended in with society and found sanctuary in the wide expanses of Nebraska, Oklahoma, and Kansas. Near impossible to find."

Lockwood clicked his tongue. "And Protection is a perfect place to hide out."

Guralnick huffed. "For years I thought I'd never see another one. But Mira, she's got a temper, and she stood out. I was able to track her to Protection."

Toby hugged Jesse to his chest. "Looks like Tagawa stirred up a whole nest of them."

"They call themselves a clan, very organized and very secretive. They have the ability to regenerate body parts, and they reproduce."

"You mean like vampires?" Stink asked. "If they bite your neck?"

Guralnick shook his head. "These Walchoks are not creatures of myth, Mister Gates. They came from bastardized science. Males and females reproduce just like everyone else, but the fetus comes out hairy and deformed. It grows quickly, sheds the hair and develops human features, completely bypassing the infant and toddler stages. Within a month they look like every other kid on the block."

"How do we kill 'em?" Toby sneered. "I want to know."

Guralnick turned to Toby. "Mister Gates, these creatures are essentially innocents. These *Walchoks* did not ask for their fate. They were born to it, due to no fault of their own. To survive they have to hide in the shadows and feed on rodents."

Toby stood. "They're dangerous and they gotta die."

"The world is filled with dangerous creatures, Mister Gates, lions, sharks, snakes, and spiders. They do not deserve to be killed simply because of what they are. Would you set out to exterminate the Walchoks just for existing?"

"No." Toby squeezed Jesse. "They deserve to be killed for what they did...to Jesse, Tagawa, and Momma...starting with Mira Lawrence. So I'll ask you again, Dr. Frankenstein, how do we kill them?"

"You can't."

"Yes we can," Stink put in. "Cut off their heads. Ask Kasumi."

Ben grumped. "This isn't the French Revolution. We are not butchers. Your best hope is to make peace with them."

At that Toby and Stink both laughed. "Can't make peace with your enemies," Stink said. "Learned that in Afghanistan."

"You gotta kill 'em to stop 'em," Toby added.

"If you don't, they come back to bite you in the ass."

"Like the Taliban."

"And the rest of them terrorist pukes," Stink spat.

"Boys." Lockwood stepped in. "Ben's right. We have to try to make peace. First thing...we've got to find Mira Lawrence. See if she'll surrender peacefully."

Toby forced a laugh. "Tell me another joke."

Lockwood opened his coat, pulled out two Alaskans, handed them to the Gates brothers. "We'll try it my way first, and if that doesn't work...we'll blow off their heads."

Toby and Stink showed their teeth. "We read you, Reid."

"Then let's saddle up."

Chapter 21

TALBOT GLANCED AT MIRA beside him, dark and beautiful as always. She sat proudly, her back straight, her hands folded regally atop her crossed knees, and her head tilted upward, obviously not intimidated by the three men sitting across from them in the Darabont mansion attic.

The men's eyes stared with a menace that Lawrence found disquieting. Mira was apparently unaffected, raising her usual impenetrable shield and staring back at the azure-eyed men with equal disdain. It would take more than this cadre from the Dodge City clan to rattle his beloved wife, who had always been the strongest in their family.

"I don't appreciate your unannounced intrusion, Mister Eisenstein. Especially at a time like this."

Talbot reached over and took her hand. "Stay calm, dear."

"You stay calm...the nerve of these bastards. My son is dead and they have the gall to come here and tell me to let it go."

Eisenstein raised a hand to her. "There's no need for hostility, Mrs. Lawrence. Please, hear us out."

"And who are these two stooges with you?"

"Gunnar and Avram. They are brothers from The Council, just as I."

Mira let out a loud huff. "You and your brothers are as welcome in my home as a termite infestation."

Eisenstein said, "Mira, please. We came to have an intelligent discussion."

"All right, Moe, tell Curly and Larry to take a hike."

Talbot squeezed Mira's hand again. "My love..."

She angled her head toward Talbot, took a breath, and then focused on Eisenstein. "Go on, then. Let's hear your plan."

Eisenstein considered her for a moment. It was widely known that Mira Goldstein had always been one of the strongest of their kind, faster, and more explosive than most, one born out of every hundred. She was especially emotional and hard to rein in when any member of her family was threatened. After the incident in Wichita when Mira nearly exposed the entire clan, The Council decided to avoid a repeat performance and requested the Lawrence family be relocated under the cover of night.

"Our safe-havens in Kansas are becoming less and less safe," Eisenstein stated. "Mira, no matter what happens, we must maintain a low profile, exist only in the shadows."

"I refuse to let my son's death go un-avenged."

"How many must pay, Mira? Mister Tagawa, Frank Rinaldi, Cassandra Gates—"

"And that's just the beginning." She would have the entire town pay by the time she was finished.

"We are hundreds in a world of billions. Obscurity is what has kept us safe from those who would hunt us down. We need to stem any further confrontations for the sake of all the clans, and for that we'll need your cooperation."

"I'm still sitting here," Mira said, "and I am still listening."

"Talbot, years ago we advised you not to run for mayor," Eisenstein said. "Being mayor, even in the flea-hole town of Protection, is not low profile."

Talbot cast a quick sideways glance at Mira. They'd had this argument before.

"My husband is a capable man, Mister Eisenstein. A born leader. He deserves to be mayor, and the people of Protection deserve his leadership.

His insistence on not expanding the town's culture into the arts and social graces is in line with the council's wishes for low-profile." She leaned forward. "And for the record, I've fought him tooth and nail on this policy, but he is more loyal to the clan than he is to my wishes."

Eisenstein studied the woman who carried herself as if she should be in charge of The Council. "And now, Talbot's secret is out. He can never go back to City Hall, and the authorities are gathering their forces to find him. His leadership is in the toilet, and all of us are now at risk of detection."

"They can do nothing to harm us."

"Easy for you to say." Talbot wagged his stub of an arm.

Eisenstein shared a look with his stooges, then: "Ben Guralnick is with them."

Talbot stared at his wife.

Mira batted her eyelashes as she recalled the old man who'd fled Darabont in fear. "He means us no harm."

"But the people of Protection do not have his same sensibilities. They can expose us, draw attention to us, and that attention will draw in the military, and they'll round us up like animals and put us back behind stone and steel walls. Do you want that to happen?"

Talbot shrank back. "No."

"Let them try." Mira scowled.

"That's not an option." Eisenstein stood from his chair. "I will escort you and your family to Dodge City. We number more than forty there. You will be safe until we can find you a new sanctuary." The lean man with dark hair gestured in the direction of the two men behind him. "Gunnar and Avram will remain, face these vigilantes, and attempt to hold them off while we make our getaway. If they cannot...I hate to think of the consequences."

Mira shook her head. "I will not run and hide."

"You will," Eisenstein said. "And you will do it now."

"And if I don't?"

"I cannot force you to come with us, Mira. I am just an advisor, hoping you will realize this move is for the common good of our kind, and for the security of your own family."

"Mira, darling..." Talbot gazed at the iridescent light that glinted from her indigo eyes. "Be sensible. If not for me, then for Ephram. He's the only son we have left."

She gripped Talbot's hand. Ephram would be safer in Dodge City, for sure. Then she would come back and knock Protection to its knees. "For Ephram." They rose to their feet. "I will find him." Then to Eisenstein she said, "We will be ready to go in twenty minutes."

Eisenstein bowed to her. "Please make it ten."

Chapter 22

MOSS HARDY BALANCED himself on the worn metal grip of his crutch and hobbled on one leg into his kitchen. He liked the stillness of his kitchen, the clock ticking on the wall near pictures of Cassandra and her boys. Here he could sit in peace for an hour or so, clear his head of all the nightmares: crunching metal, torn off limbs, and broken spines, and enjoy the warmth of the sun and the chatter of songbirds fluttering about in the backyard. Beat being dead.

Even in the dark of a winter evening, like tonight, the pot-bellied stove filled the small room with a constant glow and comforting heat. A short while ago, the sullen faces of his two stepsons had appeared at his door. Toby and Stink hadn't visited him in a month, but when they left, this evening had become anything but serene and comforting.

The fact that his beloved Cassandra had been

murdered in her room at Evergreen Gardens seemed as incredibly impossible as the world coming to an end. For a few seconds, he thought Stink and Toby were joking, but when he got a good look at the rage building behind Toby's eyes, Moss Hardy knew this was as far from a joke as anything could possibly be.

Cassandra. His life.

Gone.

Her life taken by an intruder.

Unthinkable.

He gazed out his kitchen window into the shadows. The wood in the woodpile beside his back kitchen door was nearly gone. He had been unable to split any wood since the accident, and he had too much pride to ask his stepsons to do it, so he counted on volunteers from the church. Since the weather got cold, they hadn't been very helpful.

He exhaled, turned away from the window, and grabbed his crutch. The boys were coming back for him later. He wondered when he had last cleaned his shotgun.

***

LaVertis Dixon glanced around the Comanche County Hospital Annex on his way out the door. When he arrived only minutes ago, the nurses had gathered around Haya's wheelchair with care and sincere attention. He was comforted that the old woman was in the hands of a first-rate medical team. That fact eased his guilt of abandoning the crippled woman here, even though he could not think of a single legitimate reason why she might truly need emergency medical help.

He had told the intake nurse that Kasumi's momma might have had a seizure about thirty minutes ago, and he was afraid she needed somebody better qualified than him to look after her. He knew it was a weak ploy. Haya Tagawa no more had a seizure than she had just won the Publishers Clearing House drawing.

The lie was better than leaving her alone in that motel room. Haya had agreed to go along with the ruse so LaVertis could go out to find her daughter and bring her back safely.

LaVertis dropped into his glistening black Trans Am and turned the ignition key. The muscular V8 engine rumbled under the flaming orange bird on the hood. He remembered Kasumi's voice on the phone when she called a little while ago to check on her mother. Kasumi had sounded distraught over the sudden death of Cassandra Gates, the nicest lady he'd ever met, and feared Haya might be next on Mira

Lawrence's hit list.

Closet had spoken with her, too, and he'd since packed up his firearms and lit out toward City Hall in Protection.

That was hard enough to ignore, but when she called back and told him she and Closet, the Gates boys, and a small posse led by Sheriff Lockwood were leaving Protection and about to roll to Dodge City, he could no longer sit idly by.

This manhunt didn't sit well with Kasumi, especially since Mira Lawrence's husband had killed her daddy. She'd said she'd come to peace with that, decided violence and revenge wasn't the answer, however, not knowing Mira's next move, she had to help the posse bring the murderer to justice before anyone else died.

What a fine mess Protection was in.

He considered how suddenly Kasumi had totally captivated his heart. About a week ago, something sparked the instant he saw her. The spark exploded into a full-out flame. Some people had something downright magical about them, and Kasumi Tagawa was one of those special people. There was no way he was going to sit back here in Protection, changing sheets at the Prairie Motel and babysitting an old lady, while his girlfriend was out in the cold

November wind chasing down Cassandra Gates' murderer.

He punched a button on the car radio. *Zepplin* filled the cold morning air as the Trans Am rumbled onto Highway 160, westbound toward 283 and Dodge City.

Chapter 23

CLOSET DIXON'S GIVEN NAME was Isaac. When he was five-years-old, Mrs. Kolatzic, his elderly Polish babysitter made the terrible mistake of not checking that he was safely tucked in bed before she turned on an episode of *The Outer Limits*, her favorite TV show. Every Thursday night, when his parents went to bingo at church, Mrs. Kolatzic sat dead-center on the family sofa, her hands filled with never-finished knitting, and her eyes wide open and glued to the black-and-white images on the TV screen.

Isaac had been playing in his room and grew bored with maneuvering his plastic army men in mock battle against his rubber dinosaurs atop the bedcovers. He stepped into the hallway, intending to call Mrs. Kolatzic to bring him one more graham cracker. His eyes found the TV where a grotesque monster trapped people inside a torture chamber. The victims were scared out of their wits.

And so was Isaac.

Panic stricken, he hid inside a closet and buried himself amid three old blankets and a quilt, hoping the monster would not find him if it escaped from the TV.

Mrs. Kolatzic was in near panic when his parents got home from church and found Isaac's empty bed. His mom and dad had not only upset stomachs from the tuna noodle casserole the church provided every Thursday, and from losing every bingo game that night, but now they had lost their only son as well. Mrs. Kolatzic mumbled, "We control the horizontal. We control the vertical," to herself as she passed by the door to his hiding place while searching the house with his mom and dad. Finally, the closet door opened, and after a few seconds, he heard his dad's voice say, "Just the place I would have picked to hide."

His dad reached into the closet, plucked Isaac from the pile of blankets, and pulled him close. "What is my best buddy doing in this closet?" And with a humorous grin, he called him *Closet*. The nickname stuck.

***

Closet thought it more than a little strange to walk into the City Hall sheriff's office armed with two .45 Colt 1911 pistols tucked into belt holsters, a short-barreled 12-gauge Remington shotgun cradled across his arms, and his parka filled with as much ammo as he had time to stuff into the pockets. He stood in the doorway and watched Reid Lockwood pull out two Alaskans and hand them to the Gates boys. They thanked him and tucked the guns inside their coats.

The group drove the short distance to the Darabont mansion in two cars. Closet rode beside Moss Hardy in the rear of Reid's Crown Vic. Ben Guralnick rode shotgun. Closet had seen the elderly gentleman around town through the years, at Isabelle's Market, or sometimes just strolling Protection's sidewalks, out for a long walk with his dog, Lilly. Guralnick always wore the same long gray topcoat he had on tonight.

Closet considered himself a pretty good judge of people, not only from his days in the military, but also from running the Prairie Motel for more than twenty-five years. And while Ben Guralnick was probably a person with an honest and forthright constitution, the man also seemed to be carrying the weight of two worlds on his shoulders, and no matter how far he walked around town, that weight never got any lighter.

Moss Hardy hadn't said one word since he lowered his crutch onto the back seat floor and eased himself inside. The Gates boys spent maybe five minutes with their stepfather inside his house before they came out into the cold together and dropped into separate cars. At this moment, Hardy looked as though he might shatter into a thousand pieces if anyone dared break the silence inside the Crown Vic. His fingers tightly clutched an 8-gauge shotgun.

Closet held his own 12-gauge shotgun as the Crown Vic slowed in front of the old Darabont place and parked behind a black Dodge Viper, now illuminated by the Crown Vic's headlights.

"Looks like we got company." Lockwood shined the police spotlight on the Viper and got out to investigate.

Closet pushed open the car door and stood in the brittle night air beside Ben Guralnick and Reid Lockwood. The headlights of the Gates boys' Buick rounded the curve off Avenue M down the block. Moss Hardy pushed himself up onto his only leg and braced himself on the car door. Lilly stayed in the car.

***

Toby rubbed Jesse's ears as the little dog lay in

his lap. Kasumi was sitting beside Deputy Cole Hawkins in the rear seat of Stink's Roadmaster. The plain fact that she was Sho Tagawa's daughter gave her an in on this mission, and she looked like she might be good with a sword. Here was a tall black woman, tough enough to be a Masai warrior and raised in a Japanese family. She would be a great asset in the fight against the Walchoks.

As Stink's Buick rolled to a halt in front of the long-deserted mansion, Toby was glad that Kasumi Tagawa was on their side.

Stink left the headlights on and the engine running.

"Stay," Toby told Jesse and joined Lockwood, Closet, Guralnick, and Moss huddled together near the Crown Vic, as did Stink, Deputy Hawkins, and Kasumi. The eight-man posse stood silently in the cold as if waiting for an order from a higher authority to proceed. Toby gazed at his father balancing himself, a crutch in one hand and the shotgun in the other. He hadn't seen Moss come out of the house much in the last six months, and to see him standing tall and strong beside them felt oddly comforting. His stepfather glanced at him with the hint of a smile on his lips. Apparently, Moss Hardy was proud of his stepsons as well.

"Look." Kasumi pointed at the front of the mansion.

Two men dressed in denim jackets and dark pants were walking toward them.

Lockwood twisted the spotlight on the men and rested his palm on the handle of his police revolver. "I don't like the looks of these guys."

"They got no business here," Kasumi said. "They're trespassing on my father's land."

Guralnick whispered, "Oh, hell," or something.

Lockwood stepped forward of the group. "Let me do the talking."

Kasumi felt the slight pressure of her sword strapped across her shoulder. She watched as the two men approached, each with a friendly smile on his face.

The men stopped at the edge of the grass bordering the front expanse of scrub-filled lawn. A slight breeze brought with it the smell of mulch and wet earth. "Evening," one of the men said. "Ma'am." He tilted his head at Kasumi.

"What were you doing in my house?" Kasumi demanded.

They squinted against the bright lights. "We're hoping the place is for sale," one man said.

Lockwood shushed Kasumi. "Who are you boys?

Got some IDs?"

"I'm Gunnar. Gunnar Weismann." He gestured with one leather-gloved hand at his companion. "This is my twin brother, Avram."

Closet shifted his weight and took a harder grip on his shotgun. "You gonna arrest them, Sheriff?"

Lockwood studied the two strangers. They were in their mid-thirties, just over six feet tall, and lean, with coal black, neatly trimmed hair. He nodded toward the Viper. "Is this your vehicle?"

"Our one indulgence, Sheriff," Avram answered. "Though not the best suited car for these snow-packed rural roads."

"Where are you from?"

Gunner took this one. "Dodge City."

Lockwood tapped his revolver handle with the tip of his index finger and asked Ben, "You getting anything?"

Before Ben could respond, Kasumi took one step toward the two shady men. "Is the mayor and his wife in there?"

"Ms. Tagawa, please." Lockwood stepped between her and the two men. "I'll ask the questions."

"I don't like the smell of these guys," Moss said.

Hawkins moved up beside Lockwood and took a defensive stance.

"We believe the mayor and his wife are inside. That's why you boys are here, right? Visiting them?"

Gunnar and Avram considered the shotgun in the black man's hands, the young woman's sword, the short-barreled 8-gauge gripped by the one-legged man, and the pistols holstered on the cops' hips. Gunnar must've been the braver of the two because he spoke next. "It's an old empty house. Nobody's living in there."

"Liars," Kasumi shouted. "You dishonor your family. I know the mayor is in there. I saw him last night...in a basement room. His wife has to be in there too."

"We didn't go in the basement, lady, so cool it."

Toby stepped forward beside Kasumi, pulled his Alaskan, and angled the short barrel at the twins. They could have been the Taliban for all he cared. "Answer the question. Are they in there?"

"No need for that pistol, sir." Gunnar held his hands in the air like he was being robbed. "Let's keep cool heads about this. We're just house hunting."

Lockwood said, "Toby, put that away."

"They're protecting those killers." Toby shook the gun at them. "I know it."

Guralnick took one step beyond Kasumi and Toby, and with open palms extended, addressed the men. "Please understand, boys, this is not about you."

Avram cleared his throat. "With all this firepower pointed in our direction, it's difficult to fathom how this is *not* about us."

"Mira and Talbot Lawrence crossed the line." Guralnick studied each of the men's eyes. "We need to speak with them or all hell's going to break loose, and I won't be able to do a damn thing about it."

Toby jabbed the gun at Avram. "My momma was in a wheelchair, her legs useless. She was defenseless when Mira went into her room and killed her."

"Coldhearted bitch," Stink added.

Avram said, "That was unfortunate."

Toby squinted at him. "Unfortunate?"

"All right." Gunnar put his hands down. "We've spoken to Mira."

Toby pointed the gun barrel at Gunnar's face. "Go back in there and get that bitch out here."

Lockwood put his hand on Toby's shoulder. "Slow down."

"She killed our momma," Stink said.

"And she was my wife." Moss Hardy hobbled forward and pressed his 8-gauge against Guralnick's arm. The old man stepped aside. Hardy glared straight at Gunnar, the closest of the Weismann twins.

"Mira deserves what she's gonna get."

"We're just going to talk to her," Guralnick insisted.

"No," Lockwood said. "She's going to surrender to the law, let a judge and jury decide what to do with her."

Gunnar and Avram glanced at each other, and then back at the imposing one-legged man who faced them. "She won't agree to do either," Gunnar said. "And there's nothing you folks can do about it." He threw a dagger-sharp glare at Guralnick.

Lockwood noted how Toby's murderous gaze matched Stink's and Ben's and Moss's. Reid knew what was happening. The question was how he could have let it happen. He was practically leading a lynch mob. He had to stop a moment and think about how he'd gone from lawman to vigilante.

After one tour with the army, Reid had settled back into the small confines of Protection and decided to run for sheriff of Comanche County. He never considered moving away after that, as his life's path seemed obvious.

During any typical year, the sheriff's job, based in Protection, consisted mostly of health emergencies, a runaway horse or two, and an occasional outbreak of vandalism at the old cemetery. In fact, in the last twenty-two years, Reid had never once pointed his weapon in the line of duty. Now, he was poised on the edge of the Darabont property with his fingers ready to draw his revolver and pull the trigger on the .357, six times if necessary. This thought pounded at his temples as he stood in the cold night air, facing these strange twins from Dodge City.

Part of the reason he was here had to be his loyalty to the Gates boys, their family, and how much he had mentored them over the years. But the rest of it came from the plain fact that the calm and peaceful order of Protection, his town, had been invaded by outside forces that, if left unchecked, would upset the natural tranquility he had grown to expect over the last three decades.

Besides, sheriff or no sheriff, no man could tolerate the killing of a defenseless woman in a wheelchair, especially a woman who Reid had always liked and admired. And proving a case in a courtroom against Mira Lawrence could be next to impossible, but he had to try to bring her to face justice. Still, he imagined the incredulous expression on the judge's face just before saying, "Case dismissed." At least he'd have upheld his sworn duty to uphold the law.

He drew his revolver. "Boys. Turn around, put

your hands behind your back." He tilted his head to Hawkins. "Cuff 'em up."

"Whoa now, Sheriff...deputy." Avram fell back a step, his eyes locked on the brushed chrome of the lawman's gun. "What are you arresting us for?"

Hawkins readied the handcuffs.

"We're just detaining you...for your safety and ours. You'll sit in the squad car until we get done with this investigation."

"Witch hunt is what you mean," came from Gunnar.

Stink pulled his Alaskan. "Let me shoot 'em both."

Toby clicked back the hammer on his pistol. "Right with you, brother."

"Nobody is in the house," Avram shouted. "They left an hour ago, the whole family is gone."

"You're lying again," Kasumi said. "You—"

"No." Ben Guralnick interrupted. "He's telling the truth."

Lockwood bobbed his head. "In that case, you fellas can walk out of here as soon as you tell us where they went. If not, I'll have to arrest you for interfering with a police investigation."

Gunnar saw cold resolve settle into the sheriff's eyes. "Sorry. We can't tell you."

"Maybe a night in jail will loosen your tongue. Hawkins, you're on."

Hawkins stepped forward with the handcuffs.

Gunnar stepped back, palm forward on one hand, the other pressing Avram backward. "Mira is the matriarch of our family. We won't betray her anymore than you would betray your families. If you're smart you'll—"

Moss Hardy lunged forward. His hands reached Gunnar's throat and cut off his words. "The sheriff asked you where she went."

"Moss, let him go."

Gagging, Gunnar grabbed at Hardy's wrists with both hands but couldn't free himself from the grip of a man who'd swung an axe most of his life.

Lockwood noticed Moss had given his shotgun to Ben so he'd have both hands free to choke the crap out of that guy. "Release him, Moss."

Hardy grimaced and increased his grip until Gunnar's eyes looked as though they'd pop out of their sockets.

"Dodge City," Avram shouted. "They're on their way to Dodge City, so let Gunnar go."

Moss Hardy released his grip. "Now that wasn't so hard, was it?"

Gunnar gasped and back-stepped. His hands

went to the sides of his neck.

Lockwood put his gun away. "Hawkins, take the Gates boys and search the house."

"Yes, sir."

"Top to bottom, you hear?"

A shotgun blast rocked the night. Gunnar lifted into the air and crumpled to the ground in a spray of blood. His head was blown clean off at the neck, but a gun he'd drawn hit the ground first.

Avram raised his hands. "I'm unarmed, don't shoot."

All eyes focused on Ben Guralnick, who stood with the shotgun in his hands, white smoke swirling into the air from one of the barrels.

Lockwood snatched the shotgun from Ben. "What the hell?"

"He was going to shoot Moss in the back."

"Damn." Lockwood shoved the shotgun into Moss's hand. "You shouldn't have choked him. Now look at this mess."

Moss hobbled to Guralnick and placed a hand on the old man's forearm. "You just saved my life."

"Pin a medal on me later." Guralnick spat on the ground. "No sense going inside that old house. Nothing but rooms full of bad memories." He started back toward the Crown Vic. "We're wasting time here."

"Ben? Where do you think you're going?"

He pulled open the car door. "Doc Barnett's place first. With any luck we can get to Dodge City in less than two hours."

Chapter 24

THE ROAR FROM THE MIGHTY Viper engine thumped in Avram's ears as he powered the black convertible along the dark rural highway.

Gunnar was dead.

How could this have happened?

When he and Gunnar had left the house and saw the cars in the driveway, they'd agreed to stall them with small talk, giving the Lawrence family and Moshe Eisenstein time to increase their distance from Darabont. They'd agreed no violence, but Gunnar had lost his temper at the old one-legged man who had choked him. Avram had seen the look of murder in his brother's eye. He wanted to scream no, but Gunnar had already pulled his gun.

It all happened so fast. The sheriff had turned his back, as did the old man with one leg. Gunnar's gun flashed in the headlights...then a shotgun blast, the sickening sound of lead striking flesh, and the soppy slap of a head and face disintegrating in a red spray. The face of his brother now permanently removed from the earth.

Avram thought he was next, that the witch hunters would kill him too, but the sheriff had told him to get out of town and never come back.

For the last hour, as his hands clutched the leather-bound steering wheel, he'd pushed aside thoughts of turning around and storming back to extract his own vengeance, but he now feared the humans of Protection. He would go back, all right, but he wouldn't go back alone.

It was horribly difficult to harness his mounting rage, but he was duty bound to protect the clan, not go off halfcocked on a suicide mission. He and Gunnar had been trained to keep their emotions under control. The consequences of failing to do that became quickly evident when he'd stared down at Gunnar's headless body. And right now it was incredibly hard to believe he'd have to continue on in a world without his twin brother.

Chapter 25

MIRA HOPED THAT IF SHE PACED the length of Eisenstein's rustic den enough times, the heat pounding at her temples would fade, and her cheeks would stop burning with the fires of accelerating rage. But this was the umpteenth time around the hardwood floor, and if anything, her anger was just getting started.

She understood what Eisenstein had been telling her about keeping a low profile to maintain the overall safety of her family. However, she still didn't understand how cowering in the shadows when actually faced with a real threat was anything but destructive to the very safety they were trying to protect.

Talbot had found a way to fall asleep upstairs. Ephram was asleep as well, on the bare wood floor of a bedroom across the hall. Eisenstein's compound was crawling with members of his Council, and there was probably no safer place on earth for her family than right here, right at this moment. Maybe that should have given her some solace, or at least diminish the fury building inside her, but she welcomed the flow of energy that coursed through her body when rage begged to be unleashed.

It felt right.

It felt good.

And she'd given up trying to find ways to control it, which had proven useless many years ago.

She thought about Naomi Deutcher, her best friend in high school. Shortly after Mira moved with her family to Kansas City, she'd made a connection with Naomi, and they immediately struck up a close friendship. Naomi was the opposite of Mira Goldstein. Where Mira was outspoken, strong and confident, in both body and personality, Naomi was painfully small, quite thin, and withdrawn. She would not speak unless spoken to, and even then, words came hard for her. But Naomi appreciated the attention and genuine friendship Mira provided.

It happened after gym class. Mira had wrapped a towel around her naked, wet body and watched from the far side of the showers as Carol Burdick strutted across the tile toward Naomi who was naked and still showering.

Carol Burdick towered over the smaller girl, hands on her hips, crowding Naomi from just a few inches away. "I hear you were talkin' to Jimmy."

"He's just a friend." Naomi wiped water from her eyes.

Carol shoved her into the wall. "He's my boyfriend, so you leave him alone."

Burdick was broad-shouldered and muscular for a girl, five-foot-nine, and she probably would have been attractive if she'd lost about twenty pounds along with the arrogant smirk she had plastered across her face. Burdick looked like she might have been good at sports that required more strength than skill. She apparently had better things to do than sports, like screwing every boy in school.

Mira thought it was funny how everybody knew that Carol Burdick was one of the 'easy' girls. She was only thirteen years old and already a legend in the boys' locker room.

Naomi twisted the shower handle. The stream of water stopped. She crossed her arms across her chest and tried to inch by Carol Burdick without touching her. Naomi needed to get to her towel, which hung from a hook on the wall a few feet away.

Mira could see Naomi desperately needed to get

out of harm's way.

Burdick moved an inch to one side and blocked the smaller girl. "Are you going to keep your hands off him? Or do I have to beat you so ugly no boy will ever touch you with a ten-foot pole."

Naomi's breath was stuck in her throat, but she managed to squeak out, "You can have him."

Three of Burdick's minions dressed only in towels stepped up behind their heroine. The three girls giggled to each other, apparently overjoyed they had a ringside seat to whatever was going to happen next.

Mira thought the whole scene was ridiculous and certainly unnecessary. Girls had enough to worry about in their lives other than what boy was screwing Carol Burdick. "Leave her alone," Mira shouted.

"She's trying to steal my man."

"Your boy, you mean."

Burdick inched closer to Naomi. "So you want him, don't you? You want my man between your legs to hump you like the whore you are."

"Takes one to know one," Mira struck back, standing rock solid, her feet evenly apart, fists clenched at her sides.

Burdick turned to Mira. "What are you, the slut's friend?"

"Yes."

Naomi shuffled quickly to her towel. She grabbed it from the wall, wrapped it around herself, and ran to the changing room.

"Figures," Burdick said. "I guess the sluts in this school stick together. Maybe you should start a whore club, or something."

"Maybe you should." Mira took one step forward. "You could be president."

Burdick grinned. "What are you, a virgin or something?"

Mira stood alone in front of Carol and her slutty friends. Her mind raced with the idea of grinding Carol Burdick's face into the shower drain until her pretty nose was reduced to mincemeat. The thought made a warm spot glow in her chest. She would be doing every girl in the school a service. The boys? Not so much.

"You've had your fun, Carol. Your boyfriend is all yours. Go get dressed."

Burdick put her hands on her hips and looked Mira up and down. "You got any tits under that towel?"

That welcoming flow of energy surged through her. She wasn't supposed to let her powers show. She was supposed to put them in a metal box and keep

them locked up. Low profile. For the clan. To hell
with that now. Mira's vision blurred. She saw Carol
speaking, but couldn't hear her words. She could not
hear the showers running or the drains gurgling. A
drumming inside her temples pressed against the
sides of her head, pounding...

Carol shoved Mira. "Chicken to show me your
tits?"

Mira screamed. She launched herself six feet into
the air, twisted around, and slammed her heal into
Carol Burdick's face, driving her head backward with
a sharp crack.

The whore's body dropped to the floor and
flopped around like a fish out of water.

Her friends backed away and took off at a dead
run.

That was the last time Mira saw Naomi. She
hadn't thought about her in quite a while. But the
satisfaction of seeing Carol die and how that flow of
energy simmered into a sweet pool of ecstasy was
something Mira would not only never forget but
forever crave.

A powerful rumble came from the front of the
main house. Mira moved to the window and watched
the headlights of a black sports car screech to a stop in
the driveway.

Protection

Avram piled out in a rush, but Gunnar was not with him. Something terrible had gone wrong.

***

Moshe Eisenstein saw no hint of a sunrise over the eastern horizon as the Council members dropped into their vehicles in front of his sprawling compound. It seemed as though they might be embarking on a fanciful, point-to-point road rally, as the fifteen or so engines started and filled the peaceful, early morning air with the rumble of mechanical thrumming. But this would be no joy ride.

Avram had given them the bad news about Gunnar's death at the hands of Protection's citizens, the shotgun blast that had taken off his head, ensuring eternity for the twin brother. The clan had gathered together, and despite Moshe's reservations and insistence on restraint, the vote was nearly unanimous for revenge. Avram was more than willing to go on ahead, scout the town, and locate targets as the others organized a strike force.

Fired up and ready, they waited as Talbot Lawrence and his wife appeared in the driveway. Mira hugged him, released him quickly, and strode toward Eisenstein's black Audi sedan. She made no eye contact with him as she slipped inside the car and settled amid the cushioned folds of black leather.

Eisenstein dropped into the driver's seat and pulled the door closed. Mira's feral scent filled the interior. He turned the key and started the southbound procession of vehicles, straight toward Highway 160 and Protection, Kansas.

Fifteen minutes out of Dodge City, the symphonic ringtone of the Audi sedan's cellular connection blasted from the center-dash control panel.

Eisenstein grabbed the phone and put it to his ear. "Yes?"

Mira watched him and wondered why he didn't answer through the car's audio system. He must've been up to something secretive.

"Good." Eisenstein listened then: "Just stay out of sight." He placed the phone back in its cradle.

Mira waited. When Eisenstein failed to offer an explanation for the call, she pressed the issue. "Who was that?"

"A scout."

Mira stared at him. "And what did this scout of yours have to say that's so secret?"

"Looks like our drive is going to be shorter than we thought."

"Meaning?"

"Gunnar's killers are coming our way."

She stared out at the onrushing darkness and tried to calm the storm gathering inside. She had voted to strike back at the people of Protection, and if given the choice, rid the entire town of those murderous inhabitants, replace each one with one of their own, and live in peace again.

Eisenstein wondered what was going on inside Mira's homicidal head. The woman had been wronged, deeply, and she'd stop at nothing to make Protection pay dearly for their transgressions against her and her family. He glanced in his rearview mirror at the columns of headlights jittering in the darkness behind him. She'd used Gunnar's death to rally the clan around her. The action being taken tonight was the furthest thing from low-profile they could get. As the line of cars got closer to Protection, the stronger the tingle of instinctive alarm grew at the back of his neck.

From the beginning, when he assumed the role of clan protector from his father, Eisenstein always tried to reason through problems logically. The best analytical formula was simple: balance potential gains against potential losses. Avoid violence at all costs. Yes, clan families were born from violence, and their beginnings were hushed secrets, only told to their offspring once they had aged enough to appreciate and understand their lot in life.

He glanced to Mira. She was a very real threat to the security of the entire clan. The day might not be far off when more clan members decided to follow her lead and proudly emerge from the shadows to assert their entitlement to exist in a society where they could live according to the natural selection of their birthright. Survival of the fittest would reign supreme over the land. The human race would eventually be extinguished if Mira had her way.

What Mira failed to understand about the human race, or what she underestimated, was mankind's propensity for violence, to destroy what they did not understand and to enslave and torture their enemies without mercy. The human race also outnumbered the clan by millions to one. Eisenstein shivered. An all-out battle with the rest of the world could very well mean the end of the clan's existence.

So he'd brought her along in his car for the sole purpose of keeping a close eye on her. Even now, quiet and exhibiting no emotions, Mira's internal volcano was never completely dormant, and it was just a matter of time before she erupted.

If ever there was a true example of a *force of nature*, Mira fit that description perfectly.

He thought about the dangerous course they had taken while the procession chewed up the miles toward Protection. If he didn't act soon, it would be too late to turn around. A negotiated settlement to this dispute could save a lot of lives. He grabbed his phone from its cradle and pressed one button. "I'm going on ahead. Hold back until I signal."

"What are you doing?" Mira spat.

He reset the phone, gripped the steering wheel with both hands, and mashed his foot on the gas pedal. "You'll see."

The black sedan surged forward down the dark backcountry road.

***

Talbot remembered Mira telling him to stay put and wait for her return. Stay put, like a good little boy. Like a good little dog.

A dog.

Talbot Lawrence fishtailed the black Chevy Avalanche out of Moshe Eisenstein's driveway on the outskirts of Dodge City. Someone had been foolish enough to leave the keys in the ignition. Talbot rocketed the four-wheel-drive truck along the dark Kansas highway toward Protection.

He'd loved Mira from the moment he'd first

caught sight of her walking magically across the school parking lot. And she eventually came to love him as well. He knew that. But her absolute single-mindedness sometimes drove him to the brink of complete exasperation. She always had to do things herself, do things her way, even if those things were the wrong things to do. Now she'd instantly turned his life upside down.

Talbot took a breath and let it out slowly.

He couldn't let Mira put her life on the line for his sake and their family's protection. That was his job. Her fuse was extremely short, and she acted without thinking. She acted on emotion instead of logic and common sense. But whether she was right or wrong now, it was time he pulled his own weight in their relationship, and nothing she could say or do would change his mind about that. He would do what was necessary to ensure she looked at him with some semblance of respect, so long as they both managed to survive.

***

When his front doorbell rang for the third time in the middle of the night, Doc Barnett wondered why he had chosen to go into veterinary medicine in the first place. On his way to the door, he grabbed a tissue and blew his nose. "Damn cold." He squinted through the peephole at Toby Gates who held his mom's black-and-white mutt in his arms. Doc's first thought was the dog had suffered complications after the surgery. Damn!

He opened the door and saw Ben Guralnick was with Toby. Lilly sat calmly beside the old man, tail wagging. The sheriff's Crown Vic and a Buick Roadmaster idled at the curb.

"Toby, Ben?" Doc said with reservation. "What's up?"

Ben patted Lilly's head. "We need a favor."

"At three in the morning?" He sneezed into the tissue.

"We're in kind of a rush," Toby said.

Doc stared at him and Jesse. "Is the little guy all right?"

"Never better. Look, his belly is almost healed."

The stitches he'd put in were gone, and the incision and claw cuts looked like month-old wounds, well on the mend. "That's odd?"

"A favor," Ben repeated.

"Right. Come in."

Toby and Guralnick stepped onto the polished wood floor. Doc pushed the door closed.

Guralnick said, "We would greatly appreciate it

if you could watch Lilly and Jesse for a while."

"We're going out of town," Toby added. "Don't know when we'll be back."

"I don't run a kennel here."

"Please, Doc." Guralnick reached down and scratched behind Lilly's massive head.

"Mind telling me what's going on, then?"

"My momma...she's been murdered and we're going after the killer."

Doc blinked twice. "Cassandra? Dead? I'm so sorry, Toby. What happened?"

"We don't have time to explain." Ben looked him in the eye. "Will you watch our dogs until we get back?"

"Y-yes, yes, of course. Let me make a call." He reached for the phone on the lobby counter.

Toby squinted at him. "Who you calling?"

Doc held the phone to his ear. "One of my helpers." He waited, then: "Brenda, sorry to bother you, but please get over here right away."

He hung up and looked at Toby. "Give me a minute to change clothes and grab my guns." He sneezed. "I'm going with you."

Chapter 26

IT WAS COMPLETELY dark.

He was sure his eyes were open, but he could not see even a flicker of light. He blinked, hard. Harder.

Still nothing.

Where was he? Who was he?

His breaths came in short gasps. The air was stuffy and smelled dank. He realized he was lying on his back on a flat, hard surface, and the cold seeped into every bone in his body. Not freezing cold, just numbing cold. The only sound was his heart thumping in his chest.

Panic began its lethal swim up his spine. He screamed. His voice sounded hollow and tinny and loud. He touched his chest...no shirt, his stomach...a deep hole, his hips and thighs...no clothing. How did he get naked? Instinctively, he groped the darkness, felt cold steel walls on each side of him, a cold ceiling only inches from his face. Now panic lit fires in his bloodstream. He flailed his arms, his fist pounding on metal, his feet kicking a metal barrier, and he shouted, "Somebody help. Get me out of here."

In his throes of panic, he'd struck something beside him that clattered against his cold steel tomb. That stopped him. He had to quit reacting and start thinking. What was in here with him?

He groped the hard steel beneath him, scooted sideways, and groped the darkness until his fingers wrapped around a familiar object. A sword. And suddenly he remembered who he was...and he had a good idea where he was...and he had a better idea how he'd gotten here. Now he just had figure a way to get out.

Chapter 27

DOC BARNETT STARED OUT at the darkened Kansas fields from the back seat of Stink's Buick as the car floated along Highway 160 at over seventy miles per hour. The car's ride was so smooth it was almost comforting. At any other time riding in this behemoth Doc would have been able to get some significant and immediate shuteye, but his runny nose made that impossible.

The country veterinarian pressed the top of his black Stetson tighter on his head, shifted his position, and felt the hard handle of his Taurus Gaucho pistol press against his abdomen. The Gaucho was an exact copy of an old-west six-shooter, and Doc kept the stainless steel weapon polished to a gleaming shine. He hoped it wouldn't be tarnished before this night was over.

Stink was driving the Buick just a gnat's ass

behind the bumper of Sheriff Lockwood's Crown Vic. The two-car procession raced through Ashland without hindrance of a single car or the local police. In a blink of an eye they were back on the dark highway surrounded by Kansas farmland that went on for unseen miles in the black of night.

Doc sniffed and glanced over at Moss Hardy who sat unblinking on the other side of the rear seat. Hardy had been quiet since they had all piled into the car and left Protection, and it looked as though he might shatter if anybody dared say a single word to him. The big man with one leg and an 8-gage shotgun propped in his lap looked as though he was ready to inflict serious damage on anyone responsible for his wife's incomprehensible murder.

"We're comin' up on Chadderdon," Stink announced. "Let's stop for gas at Bubs' place."

"I gotta pee anyway," Toby added.

Stink looked in the rearview mirror. He could have sworn he'd seen a flash of light a ways behind them, but in the darkness, it was hard to tell, almost as if a car was following them with the headlights off.

***

To calm his nerves, Avram fished a cigarette out of the pack in his pocket and lit it with a Zippo. The flash of light from the flame nearly blinded him. Now following the Buick across the black landscape of Kansas on this moonless, overcast night with the headlights off, his heart rate thrummed with the same rhythm as the Viper's engine.

The hardest part of the drive from Dodge City was looking to his right at the empty space in the passenger seat of the Viper. Gunnar wasn't there, no matter how many times he blinked, no matter how many times he shook his head, no matter how many times he remembered to start breathing again, Gunnar refused to reappear.

Avram's mission to scout ahead and report on the men who had killed his brother seemed a perfect fit for the mood he was in. He would be in the best position, his black car hidden under the cloak of darkness, to seek his own retribution rather than leave it to Mira Lawrence. She'd lost a son, sure enough, but he'd lost a brother. She still had a husband and another son. Avram had nothing.

He'd reached Ashland without encountering the Buick and the Crown Vic that had been parked in front on the Darabont house. He'd heard the man who'd shot Gunnar say they were headed for Dodge City. He knew they'd be along any time, so he had parked in the shadows of an Ashland alley off

Highway 160 and waited.

Sure enough, the Crown Vic and Buick had blown by like the wind was on fire.

***

Chadderdon was a pit stop at the junction of Highway 160 and 283 between Dodge City and Ashland. Eli 'Bubs' Holcomb owned the only building there, a gas and convenience store he simply called Bubs' Place. He'd gotten into work early, as he did every day, to prepare homebrewed coffee and breakfast burritos for the morning rush crowd. The place was normally as dead as a tomb at this time of morning, but in the predawn hours of this particular Tuesday, steadily approaching headlights glowed in the distance along 283 coming from the direction of Dodge City.

Holcomb wondered what would bring out such a parade of vehicles. Then, as if providence itself was shining down on him, two pairs of headlights approached from the east, coming from the direction of Ashland and Protection.

Maybe this was his lucky day. Maybe all those cars needed gas. And maybe these uncommon November travelers wanted breakfast burritos and homebrewed coffee. He needed to turn on the lights and ready the place for a whole bunch of paying customers.

The two cars coming from the east reached Bubs' Place first and pulled up to the gas pumps.

***

A hundred yards to the east, Avram coasted the darkened Viper to the shoulder across the road and killed the engine. He crushed out his cigarette in the ashtray and surveyed the lighted parking lot. From this vantage point he could clearly see the goings-on, and he knew the bright lights would make it impossible for anyone there to see his black car parked down the road.

The Crown Vic and Buick had pulled up to each of two gas pumps. His brother's killers moved about; some attended to fueling the tanks, others headed into the convenience store. The old man who'd killed Gunnar had not gotten out from either car. But Avram knew he was there somewhere.

Parked across the road and thinking about the man who had taken Gunnar's life and stewing about the empty passenger seat, Avram tried to maintain some sense of self-restraint. For the last ten years he had served the clan, and he always acted according to the rules and traditions that had kept them all safe.

But this time circumstances were different. This time he'd lost his brother. This time there'd be no self-restraint.

Avram gritted his teeth and stepped out into the frigid morning air.

***

Ben Guralnick waited in the back of the Crown Vic as Sheriff Lockwood tended to the gas pump. Ben wondered why the coldest time of a winter's day was just before sunrise. The sheriff's deputy, Hawkins, and the black woman, Kasumi, had already gotten out of the car and were walking toward the convenience store. Hawkins had stuffed his hands inside his deep green Sheriff's Department bomber jacket. Kasumi carried her sword across her shoulders like some kind of ancient warrior.

It was quiet inside the big sedan, now that Guralnick was alone, and with the engine and heater off, he quickly got cold. He removed his gloves, put both hands over his mouth, and puffed hot breath into them. He was still cold, even in his topcoat and thick scarf. With everyone out of the car, he caught a faint scent that remained.

Gunpowder.

He had fired that shotgun into the face of

Gunnar Weismann back at the Darabont mansion. That was the first act of pure violence he had committed in his entire life. It amazed him, though, how quickly he'd pulled the trigger without a moment's hesitation. He hadn't known he was capable of murder, self-defense or not.

Guralnick shivered. For all these years he had stayed alone in Protection, Kansas, secluded from most everyone. The guilt that ravaged his soul was a constant companion. He'd not only helped create the Walchoks, he had just killed one of them, and for that he would surely pay, not by man's judgment but by God's.

Toby knocked on the window and got in the back seat, rubbing his gloved hands together. "You all right, Ben?"

"I've felt better."

"Come on inside, get some coffee."

Guralnick pulled the collar of his topcoat tighter to his neck. "I would like to ask a favor of you, if you don't mind."

Toby stared at him. "I guess. What kind of favor?"

"When you go back to Protection, and you retrieve Jesse from Doc's place, please take Lilly home with you."

"Take her...what about you?"

"I fear this night won't end well for me."

"That some kind of psychic revelation?"

Guralnick put his gloves back on. "It takes no special talent to see when a man must face the consequences for his past mistakes."

Toby blinked. "If you stay in the car, there's a good chance you'll get through this night and pick up your own dog."

Guralnick smiled. "I have no intention of hiding in the car. For a long time I've kept a secret, and now that secret has been unmasked, the gravity of which has yet to be seen. A great evil will be released, and I'm powerless to stop the hell that will fall upon the good folks of Protection."

"Not if we kill the bitch first."

"It won't be that easy." Small tears pooled in Guralnick's eyes. "Sometimes we must stand in the deepest shadow to see the clearest light. And often through wrong's own darkness comes the welcome strength of right."

"Did you just make that up?"

"No. The saying has been around a long time." He clapped his gloved hands together. "So...about that favor."

Toby nodded. "Yeah, sure. If it's necessary, I will

take care of Lilly."

Guralnick nodded. "Thank you."

"But it won't be necessary." Toby left him in the car.

***

Stink sat behind the wheel of the Roadmaster and waited for the gas pump to click off when his tank was full. He couldn't remember the last time he'd slept more than an hour, but for some reason, he wasn't tired. It was tough to feel tired when thoughts of his momma's murder kept torturing his brain.

A hand rapped on his window. Closet Dixon stood outside, munching on a chocolate cupcake and staring into the distance. Stink cracked open the window.

"Think we got company." Closet pointed toward Highway 283.

Stink followed Closet's gloved finger. A pair of headlights bobbed and sparkled in the darkness, southbound and coming on fast. Behind that car, a column of headlights were proceeding southbound at a slower pace. They might have been three miles back, and he wouldn't have seen them if not for the seemingly infinite flat, treeless plains of Kansas.

"How many do you think?"

Closet took another bite of his cupcake, chewed, and squinted into the distance. "Fifteen, maybe twenty cars."

"Can't be a funeral procession this time of morning...or a Presidential motorcade."

"It's them killers coming back. What do you bet?"

Stink's chest tightened, same way it had done in Afghanistan before the first shots of battle rang out. He shoved open the door and shouted, "Hey, you guys, better take cover inside."

***

Holcomb watched customers rush toward the front door of his convenience store. He could hear the cash register ringing already. The door dinger went off as they pushed their way inside: a dude wearing a black duster and cowboy hat, a one-legged man with a shotgun, a black man with a bigger shotgun, the Gates brothers, he'd recognize them anywhere, and a tall black woman carrying a sword. A sudden fear chilled Holcomb's bones. Was this one of those smash and grab robberies? He glanced down at his old rotary-style phone, and he would've called 911 if a sheriff and a deputy hadn't followed those folks in.

Protection

***

Reid Lockwood studied his forces standing with him inside Bubs' convenience store. Toby and Stink looked itching for a fight. They'd been up all day and all night since their mother was slaughtered at Evergreen Gardens. Stink might have some veneer of self-control, but Toby's reputation for being short-tempered was well known; the story of his exploits in Afghanistan had grown to mythic proportions in Protection. Best Lockwood kept those hotheads back a ways.

"Hawkins, take the door. Moss, back him up."

At least he was still in control of this bunch, but that wasn't guaranteed to last long. Of the oddly matched gang he had with him, only Closet Dixon, Deputy Hawkins, and Doc Barnett would likely listen to his orders. Kasumi Tagawa would side with the Gates boys, whereas Moss and Ben were loose cannons. Then he realized Ben Guralnick wasn't with them. He was still sitting in the back seat of the Crown Vic. What the hell was he doing?

Doc grabbed a bottle of Nyquil from the shelf and took it to the counter. As Holcomb rung it up, Stink shoved a Big Jim's beef jerky at him, as well.

"Car comin' in," Hawkins announced. "Movin'

fast. Audi of some kind. Black. Two occupants."

Lockwood took a breath. "Crap."

"Looks like the other cars stopped down the road..." Hawkins turned back, his face scrunched up with confusion. "They just killed their headlights, sir."

Toby started for the door. "I knew we should've killed the other twin brother. The fucker called in for backup."

Lockwood stopped him. "Wait here, all of you." And pointing to Holcomb behind the register, "You too. Don't move a muscle."

***

Moshe Eisenstein parked the Audi just outside the ring of lights around Bubs' Place where Avram had reported seeing his brother's killer stop. "Hold your positions, boys," he said into the cell phone then wondered where Avram was at. The Viper was nowhere in sight. He turned to Mira. "Stay in the car."

Mira gritted her teeth. "I didn't come all the way down here to stay in the car."

He pushed a switch on the dash and silenced the engine. "And I didn't come here to argue with you." He unclipped his seatbelt and angled toward Mira.

"Those Protection folks drove a good distance in the dark of night to find you, Mira. They either want you dead or in jail. Any chance I have to settle this mess without violence will vanish if any of them sees your face. Understand?"

"What makes you think I want to settle this mess without violence?"

Eisenstein swallowed. "You won't be doing any of us any favors by poking a stick in that hornet's nest."

"They killed Gunnar. They tried to kill my husband...twice. None of them deserve to live another minute."

"Then give me that long, at least, Mira. I'll talk to them. Meanwhile, stay in the car."

"I'm not a dog you can command—"

"Please stay in the car," he whined for her benefit.

Mira folded her arms across her chest and grumped, "Fine."

Eisenstein slapped the Stetson on his head then opened the car door and stepped outside onto the dirt shoulder. He could only hope the Protection people felt like talking first and shooting later.

**

"A man just got out of the Audi," Hawkins reported. "He's standing by the road and looking this way."

Lockwood joined Hawkins at the door. The man he was referring to stood a few inches above six feet tall. He was lean with sculpted cheekbones and wore a full-length storm coat, black leather with a fur-trimmed collar. Like Doc, he wore a black cowboy hat. He looked to be unarmed, but he probably had a concealed weapon. "Let's go see what he wants." He turned back to the others. "Cover us."

"I'm going with you." Toby drew his Alaskan.

"I need cooler heads out there than you boys got on your shoulders. You're staying here."

Stink grabbed Toby's arm. "Play it his way for now. If it goes south, we'll jump in, okay?"

Toby glared at his brother and didn't say anything.

Doc chugged Nyquil from the bottle.

Moss Hardy gritted his teeth and stared at the floor. "I'll cover you from here, Sheriff. Can't move too fast on this one leg."

Doc said, "I'm coming with you, Reid." He gripped his Taurus Gaucho pistol in front of him.

"Put it away, Doc, but keep it handy."

Closet stepped up, shotgun in both hands. "I'm

coming too. Won't nobody argue with a man holding a shotgun."

"I don't want any guns visible unless it's absolutely necessary. Got it?"

Nobody answered in the affirmative.

Closet shoved the shotgun up his right coat sleeve and gripped the end of the barrel with a gloved hand. "Good enough?"

"All right. Doc, Hawkins, let's go." Lockwood pushed open the front door and stepped out into the bitter cold.

The man on the road started walking toward them, his breath vapors a mist shrouding his face.

Lockwood gritted his teeth, shoved his hands into his jacket pockets, and stepped forward with his companions, Hawkins on his right, Doc and Closet on his left. They met under the lights of the paved lot, not ten feet from the front door and ten feet apart.

"Gentlemen." The man touched the brim of his hat.

Doc did the same, like two gunfighters at the OK Corral.

Lockwood stared at the man for a moment, then: "Who are you?"

"Name's Moshe Eisenstein, Sheriff. I'm here to speak for Mira Lawrence."

"Is she going to turn herself in peacefully?"

"I have little control over my companions who are waiting just down the road. I have even less control over Mira Lawrence. She only wants to live in peace."

Lockwood squinted. "She killed Cassandra Gates. We have witnesses. She's got to face the music. Let a jury decide if she lives in peace or in prison. Got it?"

Doc sneezed.

"I have a counter offer." Eisenstein pointed to the dark highways that forked away from Chadderdon. "If you take your people back to Protection, my friends and I will return to Dodge City."

"And if not?"

"Then I will let Mira get out of my car, and I guarantee to you gentlemen..." He poked a finger at Hawkins, Doc, and Closet. "You will live to regret it, but only for a short time."

Lockwood glanced at Hawkins, who was shivering in the single-digit temperatures. Doc Barnett stood rock-solid still, seemingly impervious to the cold, gripping the butt of his gun under his coat. Closet stood stiff-armed, his white rimmed eyes staring at Eisenstein. None seemed to be in the mood to turn tail and run back to Protection.

"We're not leaving without Mira. Tell her to get out of the car with her hands in the air."

"She only gave me one minute to persuade you to leave her alone." He looked at his watch. "Time's almost up."

"I was thinking exactly the same thing."

***

Ben Guralnick remained seated in the Crown Vic as he watched Sheriff Lockwood and his companions speak with the black-clad man. Ben had a sense for recognizing Walchoks, and this time there was no question. He could smell the flowery scent of the man standing across the parking lot. He was no doubt the leader of the clan Ben had been hoping to locate.

It had already gotten icy cold inside the dark sedan. He could see his breath vapors as he watched the events unfolding only a few yards away. The fate of Reid Lockwood, a man he truly cared about, might be decided in the next minute. The sheriff seemed unsteady on his feet and looked unsure about what to do, while the young deputy seemed ready to sprint back into the store at any second. Only Closet Dixon and Doc Barnett showed no trace of fear on their faces. Maybe they had seen a great deal worse than what they might be facing now.

Ben felt compelled to do something to intervene, perhaps as a mediator between the Walchoks and the humans. Who would be better suited for the task? He placed one gloved hand on the car door handle. Maybe his life, from a young boy in a concentration camp until now, sequestered in Protection, Kansas, with a loving pit bull as his most constant friend, had all led to this moment and what he would do next. Perhaps God would then judge him at the end of his days by the actions he took now and not by the dreadful things he had done in the past.

Guralnick straightened his back, took one long breath, and opened the car door.

***

In the silence, Lockwood felt of rush of imminent dread wash over him. At this instant, he had absolutely no idea what to do. An army of these unpredictable creatures from Ben Guralnick's past were gathered a few hundred yards down the road, and probably the worst of them, Mira Lawrence, who had executed Cassandra Gates, was sitting in the Audi not ten yards away. To back off meant lives saved. To pressure for an arrest meant lives lost.

A car door opened and closed. He afforded a glance toward the gas pumps. Ben Guralnick approached, hands in his pockets and doom in his eyes.

In that moment of distraction, Eisenstein had disappeared.

Hawkins yelped.

Lockwood twisted to his right. It seemed impossible, but Eisenstein had Hawkins in a neck-lock from behind. Doc Barnett and Closet Dixon jerked their weapons free and aimed them straight at Eisenstein.

"Rein in your men, Sheriff," Eisenstein said. "This is only a demonstration of what powers you are truly up against. You cannot win. Go home and live."

Lockwood's eyes were open so wide the cold rushed in to freeze his eyeballs. Hawkins' expression mirrored his own.

"Stand down," Lockwood ordered his men.

Closet and Doc lowered their weapons. Doc sniffed.

In a blur, Eisenstein vanished from behind Hawkins and was now standing back where he started near the car.

"Hawkins," Lockwood said. "Are you okay?"

Hawkins cleared his throat and found his breath. "We should let her go, boss."

Ben Guralnick stepped up beside Hawkins.

"That would be the smart thing to do."

Doc looked shaken. "Cassandra wouldn't want us to get killed over her murder."

"Some things we can't make right, Sheriff," Closet said.

"Listen to your men, Sheriff," Eisenstein put in. "Our kind is endowed with extraordinary abilities. My strength is greater than many grown men and I have tremendous healing properties, but I am just a mouse compared to Mira Lawrence. Your time to decide is up."

"You've made my decision for me," Lockwood said.

"They're monsters." Hawkins took a step back. "Let's get the hell out of here, Reid."

"Hold your ground, men." Lockwood pulled his gun. "Moshe Eisenstein, you're under arrest for assault on a police officer."

Eisenstein shot him an incredulous glare.

"You have the right to remain silent."

"Monsters don't get Mirandized," Hawkins shouted.

Ben stepped in front of Lockwood. "Don't do this—"

With a rush of wind and the distinctive thump of flesh against flesh, Ben was suddenly propelled into the air and straight across the parking lot toward Bubs' convenience store front window.

***

Holcomb stood by his front window and watched the four heavily armed strangers outside talking with some dangerous looking dude in a long black coat. It appeared the armed men began arguing among themselves when a sudden blur sent the only unarmed man flying backward through the air. Holcomb dove to the side just as the man crashed through the plate-glass window.

Toby, Stink, and Kasumi turned away to avoid the onslaught of flying glass as Ben Guralnick exploded through the window and slammed into the metal shelves stacked with canned goods. The clatter of glass and cans hitting the floor lasted so long they thought the noise would never end.

One-legged Moss got bowled over in the process. "God damn! What the fuck was that all about?" By the time he rolled over and pushed canned goods out of his way, he got his answer.

A man straddled Ben and was beating his face with both fists. "You killed my brother, you motherfucker."

Ben's head slammed back and forth with each

blow, like his neck was broken.

Lockwood rushed into the store and tackled the attacker, who kicked his way free and disappeared in a blur before Toby or Stink had time to aim their guns.

Lockwood knelt to Ben and checked his neck for a pulse.

"Should I call 911?" the store clerk asked.

"No, he's gone. Besides, I haven't secured the crime scene. We're on our own out here."

Holcomb rubbed his arms against the invading cold air. He was living a nightmare that came to life. "I ain't never seen a dead body before."

"My God," Kasumi said.

"Who was that guy?" Holcomb asked.

Stink stared at Lockwood. "He's one of those twins from back at the Darabont place, done tossed Ben like he weighed no more than two loaves of bread."

Lockwood's eyes narrowed. "Avram got his revenge against Ben for killing Gunnar."

Stink said, "You're not gonna let him get away with that, are you, Reid?"

Lockwood gritted his teeth and remained silent.

"No," Toby said. "He ain't."

The room was quiet.

Lockwood raised his eyes and stared up at Toby and Stink. "Make sure your pistols are loaded."

"They are," Toby said.

By now Doc and Closet were standing over him. "What the hell happened?"

Lockwood stood. "Moss, are you okay?"

He was shuffling through debris in search of his dropped crutch. "Don't kill the bastards without me." He still had hold of his shotgun.

"Doc, Closet, are you locked and loaded?"

They nodded. Doc blew his nose.

"Then come with me."

Deputy Hawkins looked frightened out of his mind. "Think this through, boss. We can't win."

"Yes we can. And we will."

Kasumi said, "I'm coming, too."

Lockwood looked at her and her drawn sword. "I suppose you are."

"Reid, wait," Stink said.

"Shut up, Stink," Toby said. "We're gonna go kill us some monsters."

Lockwood let out a long breath, turned from Stink and the others, and strode deliberately out the door and into the parking lot.

This time Eisenstein wasn't standing there, and the Audi was long gone.

Chapter 28

SHE WAS BLIND. What a horrible nightmare.

Moving. A thump. Another. Thumping.

She blinked and rubbed her eyes. Nothing. No light.

Vibrations all around her, and rocking.

She took a breath. The air tasted foul.

Music, and not far away. Somebody was singing. A man. No humming. No, not either, but the whine of tires on a highway. A familiar sound.

Her brain swirled with memories. Her room...where was it? A man...who was he? A beautiful woman...pain.

She swallowed and tried to focus.

She was stretched out flat on her back.

Something was touching her face...and her bare feet. Her toes pressed against a cold blanket.

She reached out her arms and clawed at the

blanket, tore it away.

Light. Dim light, confined light.

She pushed herself up and glanced around.

She was on a gurney in an ambulance. But where were the tubes and machines? Where was the paramedic? Why was she in the back of the ambulance by herself?

She blinked. Maybe it wasn't an ambulance. She was facing the rear of the vehicle, bare metal walls, a van, hollow and metallic. Distant headlights shown through the glass of a small back window. Chrome levers for a back door latch. She swung her legs around and touched her feet to the cold metal floor then looked down at the powder blue flannel dress she always wore...but where? And how did the hole get in it, and what made the huge red stain around the hole?

"My God." She gasped. It all came back to her, the woman, the sharp bone that came out of her wrist, the excruciating pain. Then nothing.

Had she died? But she wasn't dead. But someone thought she was dead. Maybe this was a coroner's van...on the way to the morgue...the cemetery...to be buried alive. The thought froze the breath in her lungs. She had to get out...but how?

Lights swept through the interior. The sound of a

car whizzing by reached her. She turned around and moved to a wire-mesh partition that separated the driver's compartment from the back of the van. A man with buzz-cut hair was driving. Highway lane markers flashed in the van's headlights outside the windshield.

She pounded on the metal barrier. "Hey!"

The driver flinched.

"Back here!"

The man in the front seat stared into his rearview mirror with wide eyes. The van swerved into the next lane, and jerked back, tires screeching. She almost fell over, and then realized she was standing on legs that hadn't worked in six months, legs paralyzed in a car crash. She wasn't only alive, but she was alive and well. "Let me out of here!"

"Christ!" she heard him shout. The van fishtailed back and forth then left the highway, slamming into the gutter with a bone-jarring impact that tossed the van up and flipped it over.

Metal crunched and glass exploded. She was thrown to the ceiling, thrown to the cot, rammed against the back and thrown to the front. The van came to grinding halt on its roof.

She staggered across the ceiling, found the chrome lever on the back door and shoved it up. It wouldn't move. She tried again and again, until she realized the van was upside down, so she shoved the lever down and the back doors popped open. Cold air rushed in. She leaped out into the darkness, landed on her bare feet and started running across a cropped corn field.

Direction meant nothing. She ran blindly as if driven by a maternal force towards her two boys, somewhere out here in the middle of nowhere.

Chapter 29

AVRAM SPRINTED FROM THE convenience store, through the cropped fields along the highway, and back to his black Viper parked on the dark shoulder. Breathless, he dropped inside the car. Eisenstein would be furious that he'd interfered with the negotiations, but he knew with absolute clarity that the opportunity had presented itself to take down his brother's killer, and Avram had acted accordingly. Eisenstein would understand eventually, after he had some time to cool off.

He blinked and realized his heart was beating heavily from the excitement of tossing that old man through the air with no more than a casual flick of a wrist. Avram glanced at his empty passenger seat again and imagined his brother sitting there. "I got him, Gunnar. I broke his fucking neck."

Those other trigger-happy idiots had no idea

what forces they would unleash, and they too would pay their dues in the end...with their blood.

He flexed the fingers on both hands and felt a rush of strength course through his muscles. These were the hands of vengeance, and vengeance felt supreme. He started the car and powered toward Chadderdon where he turned left on 160 southbound to put himself in a different position for the upcoming battle. As he passed Bubs' Place, everyone was inside, probably licking their wounds.

***

About a mile from Chadderdon, Talbot came upon a line of vehicles parked along the dark shoulder of Highway 283. He recognized them as the cars that had left the driveway of Moshe Eisenstein's complex. Tires crunching dirt, he pulled to the roadside, his headlights revealing armed men standing about in the dark, smoking and talking. They all started yelling at him to turn off his lights.

Eisenstein's Audi pulled up across the road. He doused his lights as well.

Talbot got out and moved to meet Moshe who was already out of the Audi and grilling his men. "Has anyone seen Avram?"

Talbot shook his head. "Don't know."

Eisenstein kicked the toe of his boot against the hard ground. "Damn him."

"What is it?"

Eisenstein glanced at Mira who was staring at Talbot as she stormed toward him. He looked to be in deep shit with her.

"I told you to stay at the house," she screamed.

"I'm not going to sit around while you're out here causing who knows how much trouble."

"You're supposed to be watching Ephram."

"He's sleeping and there are several women there with him."

"We have only a few minutes," Eisenstein said, "before the Protection people launch an attack against us."

"Let them come on," Mira shouted then took one of her husband's hands. "It was brave of you to join us here. But our son, Talbot. Our son. He'll need a father if something happens to me. We both can't be at risk."

"You should be home, and I should be risking my life instead of you. Men do that for their women, you know."

"Talbot, this is no time to be romantic."

"Listen up, people."

They both stared at Eisenstein.

"Avram has suddenly escalated this misunderstanding to an all-out war."

"How?" Talbot asked.

"We should expect an attack from seven citizens of Protection, including Protection's sheriff." He blinked and shook his head. "Especially from Protection's sheriff. He's dead set on arresting Mira, and me too now."

Mira stepped in front of the men gathered around. "Could they be so ignorant? They have seen our powers and must realize how the odds would be stacked against them."

Eisenstein shrugged. "I was hoping to avoid violence."

Mira tilted her head at him. "What's wrong with violence?"

"They seem to want it now, especially since Avram screwed up our little powwow and killed the old man Ben Guralnick."

"You knew him?" someone asked.

"He's been observing us for some time now."

"How do you know he's dead?"

"I slipped into the store and checked on Guralnick so fast none of the others knew I was there."

"The name sounds familiar," another piped in.

"Wasn't he working with Major Walchok back in the concentration camp?"

"He was just a boy back then," Eisenstein told them. "Trying to survive the unsurvivable."

"He made a deal with the devil to do it," another shouted.

"Tonight he paid for his crimes against us. That, however, doesn't change our present situation."

"Let's not wait for them to come to us," Mira shouted. "Let's take the fight to them. Everyone leave your cars here and scatter into the fields. We'll meet up on the west side of Bubs' Place. Stay low, there's little cover out there."

"Wait." Talbot took her by her shoulders. "Why do you have to lead them into battle?"

She didn't say anything but glared into his eyes.

"All these years, Mira, and nothing ever changes with you. Always taking charge."

She grinned. "Perhaps that's why you love me, Talbot."

"Our love didn't start out that way."

"It's the way it is now."

"Stay here, let the men handle this. I'll go with them."

"I'll be fine, and I'll be back as always."

"I'm going with you."

"No." She glared at him. "Write some more poetry and let me handle the killing, my love." She sealed her snide comment with a kiss on the cheek.

He forced a smile only because he knew he couldn't win this argument anymore than Protection could win this war.

She slipped into the darkness beyond the line of cars at the edge of the road. Talbot chased after her.

Chapter 30

IT APPEARED AS THOUGH Eisenstein and his Audi had disappeared into thin air.

"Reid," Stink said. "Where did they go?"

"Son of a bitch."

Toby shouted, "We gotta go after them."

"Not out there in the dark." Lockwood holstered his gun. "Here we have light, shelter, food and water. They'll be back."

"What makes you so sure?"

"Mira wants us off her back and she hates to lose."

"We're not sure what we will be facing," Doc put in. "All those men with supernatural powers against the seven of us regular Joes."

"Remember the Alamo," Closet put in. "Bad odds then too."

"Come on, Closet," Toby said. "Everybody

knows the underdogs lost that battle."

"Okay, but still..."

"Let's get back inside." Lockwood led the way.

Toby and Stink stayed outside.

Holcomb had found a blanket to put over Ben, head and all now covered, and then started picking up the place. "Sun should be up in two hours. People will be showing up. What am I gonna do? What am I gonna say? 'Just walk around that body on the floor. Everything is okay, folks.' Well, I'll tell you, Sheriff, none of this is okay."

Outside, Toby leaned against Stink's Roadmaster still parked at the gas pump and opened the chamber on his Ruger Alaskan. "If that bitch gets away again..." He gazed at the .454 Casull shells that filled the cylinder and thought to etch Mira's name on all six of them.

"She won't." Stink faced him. "We're military, Toby." His breath puffed white in the morning air. "When you plan a military attack, you first judge the enemy's strengths and weaknesses."

Toby gritted his teeth. "Ex-military."

"We need somebody on recon."

"Lota good that'll do without night vision goggles."

"Yeah." Stink removed the Big Jim from his

pocket and peeled back the wrapper. "Want some?"

Toby declined.

Stink tore off a chew.

A car engine's rumble came from Highway 160, two headlights racing in from the east. The car careened into the light of Bubs' Place and screeched to a stop. It was a glistening black Pontiac Trans Am.

"I'll be damned," Stink said, chewing beef jerky.

Closet burst from the store. "I don't believe it."

LaVertis Dixon bailed out of the muscle car and straightened up. He spotted his poppa, smiled, and pushed the car door closed behind him.

Kasumi charged out the convenience store in disbelief. "What are you doing here, LaVertis? You're supposed to be watching my mother."

"Kasumi." LaVertis lugged toward her. "She's fine."

They embraced in the parking lot.

"Guess I got here in time," LaVertis said. "So what's happening?"

"We're waiting," Toby said.

"For what?"

"All hell to break loose. What else?"

"You shouldn't be here, LaVertis," Closet said. "Go back and watch the motel."

"I'm not going back, poppa. My place is here

with Kasumi. You go watch your own motel."

"Now LaVertis," Kasumi said, "don't be that way. You should honor your father and do what he says."

"I just wanta make sure you're safe for your momma's sake. What kind of trouble are we up against here?"

"About fifteen cars full of trouble, boy," Closet said.

"Jesus." LaVertis glanced at Toby and Stink. "Well, all the more good reason for me to be here."

He glanced around at all his armed friends gathered in the frigid air as if getting ready to march straight into battle. Judging from the firepower he saw, the people in those fifteen cars had better be ready for one serious fight.

"Where is my mother, LaVertis?"

"She's in good hands at Comanche County."

She tilted her head at him. "You took her to the hospital? Why? What's wrong with her?"

"They're just watching her. She's in a safe place. I had to come here, Kasumi. Couldn't bear to think my girl was in danger and I was doing nothing about it."

"I'm not your girl."

Stink winced, tore off another chunk of jerky.

"You know what I mean," LaVertis said. "I

thought you'd be happy to see me." By the way his chin shuddered, he looked like he might cry at any second.

Lockwood joined them outside. "We can use the help." He pulled a shotgun from the Crown Vic, cracked it open, counted two shells, and slapped it close. "Here." He tossed it to LaVertis. "Make every shot count."

"How many are there to shoot at?"

Closet shrugged. "An army. Is that enough?"

"All those people protecting Mira? That don't sound right."

Toby jumped in, "We're not even sure they're people."

LaVertis frowned. "Not people?"

"Walchoks," Kasumi said. "Ben knows the most about them, but he's dead."

LaVertis dropped his jaw. "Old man Guralnick is dead?"

"A Walchok broke his neck."

"We do know," Lockwood said, "that you have to blow their heads off to kill them."

LaVertis stared at him. "Like Zombies?"

"Worse. Zombies are slow and stupid. Walchoks are fast and smart."

"Real fast," Hawkins added. "So fast you can't

see 'em move."

LaVertis looked worried. "Then how we gonna whoop 'em?"

Lockwood answered that one. "Ben said the only way to win was to make peace with them."

"And that's not happening," Toby assured everyone. "Mira's going down for killing our momma, ain't that right, Stink?"

"Right, bro." Stink finished off the last bit of jerky.

"Don't you boys get too cocky," Lockwood said. "These creatures are unpredictable."

"Creatures?" LaVertis said.

"But one thing's for sure. They're not giving up Mira to face justice."

LaVertis nodded to his poppa. "I better scout around, see what they're up to." He gripped the shotgun like a Comanche warrior. "Give me about ten minutes."

"Whoa there, LaVertis," Stink said, "I think you better stay here."

"No, Stink. I came down here to help. Every good soldier needs to know their enemy's strengths and weaknesses."

Stink and Toby shared glances. "You're right," Toby said.

Doc Barnett took a step toward him. "Are you sure about this? It's dangerous out there in the dark. The Walchoks could be anywhere. "

"Yeah, man. I'm sure." LaVertis glanced at Kasumi. "You stay here where it's safe."

"I'm going with you," she said.

LaVertis squinted at her. "You can't be serious."

She faced him and poked one index finger against the center of his chest. "I may not be your girlfriend but I'm with you."

He looked at Lockwood. "If you don't hear from us in ten, don't come lookin'. Just hunker down."

Lockwood nodded once. "We'll wait in the store."

***

Mira and Talbot joined the men gathered in the field west of Bubs' Place. The cropped corn stalk stubble was brutal on skin and clothing and had proven to be a major obstacle course and tripping hazard. Mira had no idea who a lot of these men were. All seemed around the same age: late 20s to early 30s. They all wore long black coats as if they were some type of uniform. The group silently watched Eisenstein as he moved to join them.

"I want no misunderstandings. These people

cannot be reasoned with. We're not giving up Mira, so they all must die before we can slip back into the shadows and live in obscurity."

"They've forced us to take this action," Mira said to the group.

Talbot backed her. "And that is exactly what we shall do. Fight back."

"Most of you have experience with firearms. We have limited ammunition so don't waste your shots."

"Guns are ridiculous." Mira raised her right arm. A slender bone slid free from her wrist. "Use the weapon Major Walchok gave you. Look into their eyes as you run it through their gut."

Eisenstein said, "Those people are armed with weapons that can strike from a distance and kill us, Mira, if their bullets are well-placed. You may not get close enough to use your wrist fangs."

She angled back from him. "We are faster than their bullets. Stay alert. Stay alive."

Eisenstein gritted his teeth, then: "Choose your weapons, use them carefully. Before the sun rises we will win the day and put this regrettable business behind us."

Mira didn't say anything, but if she had her way, they would own the town of Protection before the next sunset.

Chapter 31

LAVERTIS EDGED QUICKLY through the cornfield furrows, trying to move as noiselessly as he could. He paused a few times to look back and make sure Kasumi was still there. She moved through the clumpy dirt and chopped corn stalks with hardly a single crackle underfoot. Her daddy had taught her to be light on her feet.

He stopped near the end of an overhead irrigation rig. Kasumi crouched and settled beside him behind a knobby, mud encrusted tire. By the distant light of Bubs' to the east, he could barely make out a group of dark-clad individuals about fifty-feet away. A man who looked to be in charge was dividing the group with hand signals and pointing in directions they were to go. It looked like they planned to surround Bubs' Place and attack from all sides.

Kasumi whispered, "I counted thirty-five of

them."

"They—" LaVertis heard a rustle behind him. He angled his body and glanced backward. A silhouetted man stood watching them from twenty feet away. He was tall, dressed in black, and looked much like those in the field. LaVertis's heart thumped with dread. He touched Kasumi's arm and pointed over her shoulder.

She turned. "Shit!"

The man held them at gunpoint. "Get up, real slow like."

LaVertis and Kasumi slowly stood and faced him.

"Drop your weapons," the man said.

LaVertis slowly set down his shotgun, careful to keep the barrel out of the dirt. "Look, mister, we don't want any trouble, just out to do some bird hunting...once the sun comes up."

"With a sword?" He waved the gun. "You too, lady. Drop it."

She complied, slowly.

"You think I don't know who you are?" He stepped closer, a bit unsteadily on the loose soil. "We've met before..." His gun was pointed at Kasumi. "At the Darabont mansion where your people killed my brother."

LaVertis edged in front of her. "We don't know

anything about your brother. You have us mistaken for someone else."

He raised the gun, straight-arm at Kasumi. "The look in her eyes was unforgettable... when my brother's head was blown off right in front of me. You, sir, weren't even there."

Kasumi nudged LaVertis aside. "Your brother pulled a gun on us. Mister Guralnick fired in self defense."

He raised his free palm to her. "He has paid the ultimate price for murdering my brother, so the question is whether or not you two are prepared to do the same." Avram took one step toward Kasumi.

LaVertis had no clue what this character intended, but from the look in his eyes, a friendly handshake wasn't among the possibilities. "Stop."

In the blink of an eye, Avram chopped the butt of his gun across LaVertis's forehead, dropping the big man to his knees then slamming him to his back in the dirt.

LaVertis's breath huffed out.

Avram dropped and rammed his knee into the fallen man's breastbone.

"No, mister, don't," Kasumi shouted from behind him.

Avram had LaVertis pinned, though LaVertis

pushed back with his hands on Avram's chest. "My foolish friends are going to attack your people with guns." He dropped his gun in the dirt and raised his arm. With a squishing sound, a poker slid out of his coat sleeve, black and drippy and illuminated by the distant lights of Bubs' Place. "But I prefer using the weapon I inherited from my creator."

LaVertis's eyes were ringed in white and bleeding terror.

"Eisenstein has forgotten his heritage...huh!" Avram's eyes popped wide open, his face suddenly creased with pain. He stared down at his midsection where the last few inches of a Samurai sword stuck out just under his sternum and gleamed with crimson blood. The look on his face turned to disbelief...then he toppled to the dirt.

Kasumi retracted the bloody sword and stooped to LaVertis. "Are you all right?"

He shook his head. "That guy was strong as an ox. If the rest of them guys work out like him, we don't stand a chance." He struggled to his feet and picked up his shotgun. "We have to get back and warn the others."

Kasumi stood. "They know."

"Are they nuts?"

"Revenge knows no common sense." Kasumi

took LaVertis's right hand. It was covered in blood. "Sorry about this."

LaVertis examined his fingers. They were all there, but two were badly sliced. "You nicked me with your sword."

"You should have moved your hand." Kasumi stepped up to Avram Weismann, crumpled in his deadfall. She gritted her teeth, tapped her sword on his neck then slowly lifted the blade straight up above her head.

"Whoa, whoa there," LaVertis said.

"I have to finish him."

LaVertis stared down at the man on the ground. He was curled into a fetal position. His hands and feet were still twitching.

"Finish him? You ran him through, Kasumi. He's gonna bleed out and die any second."

"You don't understand —"

"Hey, hey. Is that the guy who killed your poppa?"

"I'm going to cut off his head. I've got to."

Avram stopped twitching.

She held her breath and reared back with the sword.

LaVertis grabbed her wrist. "See? What'd I tell ya? He's dead."

She stared at LaVertis.

He lowered the sword for her. "You're not that kind of woman."

"But..."

"We gotta report in." He took her by her shoulders and turned her back toward Bubs' Place.

***

LaVertis and Kasumi stepped over the broken front window sill and into the convenience store where the air was just as cold inside as it was outside.

Lockwood faced LaVertis. "What did you see?"

"Counted thirty-five of them fanning out, maybe a few more." He set the shotgun on the counter, earning an odd glance from Holcomb at the register. "They got plenty of guns. I 'spect they'll attack from all sides at once."

Toby blinked. Kasumi's sword sparkled with blood. "What happened?"

"Avram was out there," she said. "Caught us from behind."

"The guy got the best of me," LaVertis added. "Musta worked out at the gym a lot. Some sharp poker came out of his coat sleeve, never seen a weapon like that before, some Ninja thing, I guess, but she killed him, saved my life."

"Not exactly." She hung her head.

Toby whistled. "You couldn't do it, could you?"

"I wanted to. LaVertis stopped me."

"She was going to cut his head off. That's not like her—"

Toby grabbed LaVertis by the coat collar and shoved him against the counter. Cigarette packs went flying. "You fool."

"He was dead. She ran him through with her sword." LaVertis offered up his cut fingers as evidence. "Even nicked me doin' it."

Closet grumped. "You should'a let her finish him, son."

Hawkins got in LaVertis's face too. "Thanks to Avram, Ben Guralnick is chilling in the beer cooler right now."

"And that poker wasn't a Ninja weapon that came out of his coat sleeve, you idiot." Toby wanted to bitch-slap him. "He's a monster like the rest of them, and he's not dead until his head is cut off."

"Shit," Doc said and sneezed. "We could've been less one Walchok to worry about."

Stink spat. "Now he's probably up and about and having one hell of a laugh with his friends."

LaVertis glared at Kasumi. "Why didn't you tell me that?"

"You didn't give me a chance because you think I'm some kind of angel. Well, I'm not. Not anymore." Tears flooded her eyes. "I'm not." She sank to the floor, sobbing. "I'm not."

"Reid," Doc said. "We came here for Mira Lawrence, not to face an army of monsters. I say we retreat." He blew his nose.

Toby let go of LaVertis and faced Doc. "There'll be no retreat."

Lockwood felt his stomach scrunch between that proverbial rock and a hard place.

"Look." Holcomb produced a Glock from under the counter.

Everyone looked at him.

"No, don't look here, look out there." He pointed to the parking lot.

Lockwood followed Holcomb's index finger. An arcing line of Walchoks, all dressed in black, walked deliberately toward the convenience store, all plainly out in the open within the circle of lights. "What the fuck are they doing?"

"Surrounding us." Toby drew his gun.

All eyes stared outside. Nearly everyone was paralyzed by the terrible spectacle. Arm after arm rose up and pointed gleaming silver handguns and black barreled shotguns straight at Bubs'.

"Reid," Hawkins said from the front door. "I strongly suggest everybody get down on the floor."

Holcomb's eyes widened. "Oh, God."

***

Mira remained still outside the lighted area around Bubs' Place and watched the cadre step toward the store. Eisenstein was afraid if those fools inside caught sight of her, they might spring into action and strike hard. So he had ordered her to stay behind and not get involved.

How dare he..?

And Talbot wanted her to stay out of it too.

Intolerable.

They wanted her and their kind to spend their lives in the shadows, low-profile...the whole idea made her sick. The entire town of Protection lay just down the road where they could live free from obscurity, walk in the sunshine, and create a life ripe with art, music, and fine dining.

A smile formed on her mouth and in her heart, and she slowly stepped out of the darkness and into the light.

***

Shots rang out like a hundred strings of

firecrackers. Canned goods and bottles exploded. Stink lay face-down on the floor and folded his hands across the back of his head. A torrent of window glass rained down. Boxes and cans on the store shelves shredded and popped from the barrage of bullets and flying glass.

And then it was over.

The gunfire stopped as suddenly as it had started. Glass fragments still clattered to the floor, as if the last of a hailstorm was leaving a bit more behind.

Stink raised his head and dared a look to the parking lot, expecting the Walchoks to be rushing in. They'd probably stopped firing because they'd run out of bullets, so any further battle would be hand-to hand combat. Surprisingly, the line of Walchoks had retreated to the edge of the lighted area, probably to reload.

He twisted and found Toby a few feet across from him on the floor, now sitting up and brushing glass fragments from his clothes. A line of blood trickled down his face from a cut on his forehead. A red circle spread on the right thigh of his canvas hunting pants. He didn't seem to notice the blood.

"Holy Mother," Closet said from the floor. He was lying on his back in a sea of broken debris and rubbing his left shoulder with his right hand.

Stink pushed himself to his feet and stepped over to Closet. "You okay, Mister Dixon?"

LaVertis scooted close to them. "Poppa?"

Closet took Stink's hand and struggled to a sitting position. "Must've used up another one of my cat lives."

Lockwood kicked broken glass with his boots and gazed out to the parking lot. "I wonder what they're doing now?"

Stink navigated through the morass to his brother, who had yet to get to his feet. "What's wrong?"

Toby shook his head. "Damn it all." He jerked at his pulverized and bloody pant leg, ripping the material in two sharp pulls. His thigh was leaking blood from an array of ragged holes. "Birdshot."

"Think you can stand?"

"They're firing turkey rifles at us?" He brought his good leg underneath him and stood but fell, groaning in pain. "I can't—"

"Hold on." Doc Barnett moved quickly to Toby, swiped glass from the tiles, and bent to the floor on his knees. "Let me look at that leg."

Stink stood and edged back against the front counter to gaze at the devastation. He shook his head, and his stomach twisted.

How had it come to this?

These were good people, and before today, he could never have imagined any of them cowering on the floor of a convenience store in a quest for justice for his murdered momma.

He took a deep breath and tried to calm himself. He needed to think, really think hard. He was smart enough to figure a way out of this mess. He took another long breath, and studied the scene in front of him.

Toby was obviously in pain but trying to soldier through it. He never liked anyone to know he was hurt, or somehow not strong, able, and willing to continue the fight. He was that way when he was a kid, and he was that way in Afghanistan. But Toby was hobbled this time, and it looked as though he would have trouble standing upright much less drawing a steady aim with his Alaskan. The very sight of his brother hurt and bleeding on the floor sent shivers up the back of Stink's neck. Felt as if the world was suddenly flipped upside-down.

Stink blinked. It was only a matter of time, probably minutes if not seconds before the Walchoks launched another assault. They'd be slaughtered this time, for sure.

Protection's only veterinarian had set a shiny revolver on the floor beside him as he attended to Toby's leg injury. Kasumi had brought him bandages and cotton balls and a disinfectant spray from the medical aisle, which was pretty much in shambles like the rest of the place. She might have been sobbing earlier, but Stink could see the rage again burning behind her eyes.

Closet Dixon was still down. He and LaVertis were trying to make quick sense of his injuries. His smile had been replaced with a blinking stare of confusion.

Reid Lockwood and Deputy Hawkins were hunkered down behind a collapsed shelving unit to keep an eye on the goings-on outside. They knew their chances of arresting Mira Lawrence were slim to none.

Stink felt pressure on one shoulder and turned to see his stepdad beside him, balanced on one crutch and a shotgun pressed close to his body under the same arm. "You hurt?"

"No, Dad. You?"

"Don't matter."

Stink noticed a blood smear on the side of Moss's neck. "You've been shot."

"Still standing. That's all that matters." Moss

took a breath. "Your momma was worried every waking second when you and Toby were gone for those war years. Was nothing I could do to get her to think of somethin' other than you two boys." He shook his head. "Truth was...I was worried too."

"I miss her, Dad. I do miss her every second."

"I'm going out there, son."

Stink shook his head. "No-"

"If we just sit here, they're going to come at us again. Toby needs a hospital. We got zero chance. There's no cover in this place. We're surrounded. Couple of us are hurt already, without ever firing a shot. Besides—"

"You're not going out there, Dad," Stink shouted.

"What?" Toby stood and dragged his bad leg to Moss and Stink. It was bandaged up around the seeping wound. "Nobody's going anywhere."

Moss gritted his teeth. "I'm gonna kill that Mira Lawrence myself. End this thing right now." He moved for the door. "I got to try."

Stink blocked him. "I'm going with you."

Toby watched the blood seep down from Moss's neck into the fabric of his sweater. "Damn." He hobbled up beside them. "Me too."

Moss raised his eyes to his stepsons. "No."

Toby stared at the big man holding a crutch in one hand and a shotgun in the other. "We know what you're feeling, Dad. We want to kill that monster as much as you do."

"Then we better get to it," Moss said.

Stink suddenly couldn't breathe. It was certain death to walk out of here and face down against those armed creatures. He'd never seen Moss lose his temper, but it appeared he and Toby were going to have a front-row view.

Lockwood stormed up to Moss and Stink. "Nobody's going out there." He turned to Holcomb. "Call 911. Tell them we need the State Police and the National Guard out here, pronto."

Relief washed over Holcomb's face. "Yes, sir." He picked up the phone. His look of relief morphed to terror. "No dial tone."

"They must've cut the line," Hawkins said.

"Damn." Lockwood got out his cell phone. *No Service.* "What the hell?"

Holcomb said, "That's why I have a land line. It's a dead zone out here in the middle of nowhere Kansas."

Moss tilted up his shotgun with his free hand. "That's it. I'm goin' out there."

"No you don't, Moss." Lockwood moved to the

door. "I'll make a break for the Crown Vic, use the police radio to get help out here."

"You'll need a distraction. Wait a sec..." Stink rummaged through store debris, came up with a long-handled snow scraper and white paper towels and duct tape. "We'll hold their fire with a white flag while you make the call, Sheriff."

Lockwood pursed his lips and nodded. "It's worth a try."

Toby collapsed to the floor. "Hurry up before I bleed to death."

Chapter 32

BRENDA HELD A FRESH MUG of hot chocolate in her hands, soaking up the heat and the aroma, and wondering why Doc Barnett kept his clinic so cold all the time. No wonder the man always had the sniffles.

She looked to the polished wood floor in the back pet playroom and watched Lilly roll around on her back while little Jesse pounced on her and nibbled at her ears. They were obviously happy to be with each other on this cold Tuesday morning. She wished the sun would come up and finally spread some warmth around Protection.

Jesse suddenly straightened up and stood still, as if a jolt of electricity had paralyzed him.

"What's up, boy?"

He dashed to the back window and struck the same pose.

"Something out there? A rabbit maybe?" She'd

said it even though she knew it was too dark for rabbits to be up and about yet. Still, Jesse's back was straight and his legs were stiff.

He woofed a little and let out a low growl.

So that was it. "You need to go outside, boy?"

He turned to her and started barking. Lilly got to her feet and ran around Jesse, either equally excited or actually trying to distract Jesse from whatever it was that had him riled.

"All right." She moved toward the door.

Jesse jumped up and down beside her as she padded across the floor.

She switched on the yard light, and as soon as she pulled open the door, Jesse charged outside. She hugged herself against the cold and stood on the concrete porch to keep an eye on the pooch. A six-foot stockade fence surrounded the yard. "Get busy, boy." She sipped hot chocolate.

However, Jesse didn't sniff around for the perfect spot to relieve himself. Instead, he planted all fours and swiveled his head from side to side. Something strange had this dog's attention.

"Go ahead, boy," Brenda said. "Go get yourself busy."

Jesse angled his head over his shoulder and studied her with his deep brown eyes. Then, as if having seen enough, he turned his head back, crouched down slightly, and leapt into the air, easily clearing the high fence.

A wave of paralyzing shock struck Brenda. She dropped her mug, and it shattered on the concrete porch. She took a breath and held it. How was she going to explain the dog's great escape to Doc Barnett? *Jesse jumped the fence.*

He'd never believe that in a million years.

***

Moss looked over Lockwood's shoulder at his stepson walking away from the storefront. Stink carried a long plastic ice scraper with a white paper-towel flag stuck to it with gray duct tape.

Standing in the framework of the broken windows, the others brandished their guns. Kasumi even had a gun: Stink's Alaskan.

Lockwood moved to his position at the front door, ready to sprint to the Crown Vic. "If any one of them Walchoks shoot, let 'em have it."

Stink walked toward the group of black-coated Walchoks. There was no doubt he had their undivided attention. He waved the white flag and hoped like hell that meant *no shooting* to the monsters.

Protection

***

Eisenstein raised a fist in the air. "Hold it."

The Walchoks stopped reloading their revolvers and waited for Eisenstein's next instruction.

Mira walked up from behind and stopped beside Eisenstein. "What's going on?"

Eisenstein glanced at her. "One of the Gates brothers."

"He has a white flag," Talbot said.

"Avram," Eisenstein called out.

"Here." Avram moved to the front. "Yes, sir."

"Shoot the bastard."

"It's a white flag," Talbot said. "You can't shoot him."

"I'm not going to shoot him. Avram is."

"Wait," Mira said. "Let's see what he's got to say."

"You just want to hear him grovel, beg for their lives. Why torture him? We'll just shoot him and be done with it."

She blinked at Eisenstein. "You heard what I said."

"Maybe they're going to surrender," Talbot said.

"We're not taking any prisoners. It's not that kind of war."

"No." Mira smirked. "We're taking the whole damn town."

"What?"

"You can't do that."

She smirked. "Watch me."

Talbot saw the familiar rage lurking behind Mira's deep indigo eyes. He had seen that look before. But it was the wan smile touching the corners of her mouth that made his stomach twist and the back of his neck prickle with icy, immeasurable fear.

Eisenstein didn't have the time or patience to argue with her. "Get out of sight before any of them see you."

"I want them to see me."

"Shit." Eisenstein stepped forward to meet the approaching Gates brother.

***

Toby aimed his Alaskan dead center on Eisenstein's forehead. "One wrong move," he muttered, "and you're a dead mother."

Kasumi drew a bead on Avram.

Doc had Mira framed in his sights and hoped he wouldn't sneeze at an inopportune moment.

Lockwood waited for Stink to strike up a conversation. Then he'd break ranks for the car.

Toby's gun hand wobbled. The tremors surging through his body came from the wound in his leg. The pain was nearly unbearable...nearly. He'd never let on otherwise. On top of those ails he was hallucinating too, evident by the distant dog barking he heard like an echo in his skull. The bark sounded like Jesse's, but it couldn't have been his because he was under Brenda's watchful eye at Doc's place thirty miles away.

Stink was easing closer to the Walchoks.

The barking was getting louder.

Toby shook his head. A black and white streak shot toward him from the left. He had only enough time to blink before he was struck center chest with the force of a cement bag. He flew backward and crashed to the floor. A wet tongue lapped his cheeks and chin.

"Holy crap." Toby gasped.

Doc Barnett stepped over to Toby and stared down at the impossible scene on the floor. Jesse was standing on Toby's chest, licking his face, hard and fast.

Toby took the little mutt with both hands and held him away from his body. He stared at the dog as Jesse's tail fanned the air. "What the hell?"

Doc crouched beside them. "Thirty miles is a

long way for a wounded dog to run."

"Look at him," Toby said. "No sign of the surgery at all."

Doc edged closer, took the dog. There wasn't even a scar. Jesse was obviously happy. His mouth was open in a doggie smile, and his tail constantly wigwagged. He set the dog on the floor. "I don't know how to explain the impossible."

Jesse fixed his eyes out the front window. He gave one *woof* and vanished from the store.

***

Stink stopped at the edge of the lighted parking area.

A man dressed in black appeared in front of him. "Mister Gates. What can I do for you?"

Stink gritted his teeth and planted his feet solidly apart. This was *his* time to step to the front of the line, to help his brother, to help his family. "We have wounded."

"Now isn't that a shame."

"My brother, for one. My friend's father for another."

"Couldn't leave well enough alone, could you?"

He tightened his grip on the ice-scraper flagpole and hoped Lockwood could make his move to the car without being noticed. Stink waved the flag. "We want a cease fire."

That got the bunch laughing.

"It's not funny." He felt something press against his ankle and braved a look down.

Jesse?

What the hell? How had the little guy..?

The mutt sat beside Stink's foot and stared past the man facing him.

A woman emerged from the group of men behind Eisenstein.

A deep, menacing growl rumbled from Jesse's throat.

"Where did that dog come from?" Mira asked.

Eisenstein turned to her. "I told you to stay back."

"The dog's staring right at me."

A shiver attacked the base of Eisenstein's spine.

"Such fury in that little dog," she said.

"It's just a dog, Mira. He's got four legs and a tail like any other dog."

She blinked. "Except..."

Eisenstein squeezed his eyes shut for a moment. "You see it, don't you?"

"He's one of us now."

"Hey, asshole," Stink called out. "Did you hear

me? We want a cease fire."

Mira stepped in front of Eisenstein. "And we want the town of Protection."

"Mira, please," Eisenstein said.

Stink didn't know what to say. Movement on his right caught his eye. Toby and Moss halted beside him. Stink looked back and saw Lockwood had made it halfway to the Crown Vic when he changed directions to join Toby and Moss.

"You can't have our town," Lockwood said to Mira and then pointed a stiff finger at the other Walchoks standing behind her. "Go back to Dodge City. Leave us alone."

Moss held his shotgun in one hand, the muzzle of the gun pointed downward. Toby's Alaskan was gripped in one hand, hanging at his side. A second later Hawkins, Doc, and Kasumi joined them, their weapons in hand but not threatening.

"Seems you all better rethink the sheriff's last statement," Stink said to the Walchoks. "But Mira Lawrence stays."

"We'd rather kill all of you," Eisenstein said. "Our existence must remain a secret."

Avram spoke up. "You know about us, you must die."

Cheers rose up behind Eisenstein.

Mira grinned her wicked grin. "There's no need for more senseless killing."

Eisenstein asked, "What do you propose, Mira?"

"I'm sick of living in the shadows. Aren't we all?" She swept a hand to her fellow Walchoks.

They nodded in agreement.

"In the old days, to save the young warriors of some tribal villages, warring factions would send just two fighters forward, the best fighters from each side. Those two warriors would battle to the death. Winner takes all."

Stink looked from side to side at his band of brothers. Toby, by far the best fighter of the bunch, was seriously wounded. The others were too old, too big and too slow, or of the female persuasion. That left only Stink to take the challenge. The benefits had to mightily outweigh the risks, so he had to ask: "If we win, we get Mira Lawrence to stand trial for murdering our momma, Cassandra Gates."

"No way, Stink," Toby shouted. "I want her head."

"Shut up, Toby." Stink nodded to Mira. "And if you win..?"

She inhaled. "We get Protection, the entire town to do with as we please."

"Innocent people live in Protection, what about

them?"

"They'll have to move or die. Their choice." She cackled.

She actually cackled. What a bitch!

"We will no longer live in the shadows."

Eisenstein spoke up. "Mira is unquestionably our best fighter. Who will you send to his death?"

Stink groaned. This was it. Time to put up or shut up. He was the only one who could save Protection and bring Mira to justice.

"Who will it be?" Mira pressed.

"That would be me," a woman's voice said behind Stink. A familiar voice.

He spun around to see his momma standing there. It had to have been a vision. Momma would never walk again, yet here she stood in all her beautiful, wonderful glory. He had to will his mouth to speak, "Momma," and threw his arms around her.

"Morgan. I missed you."

He felt his mother's arms encircle part of his middle. She rested her cheek against his chest. Her hair was a stinky blond mat, but he didn't care.

"Momma?" Toby said. She looked like she'd been dragged out from under a bus.

She turned her eyes to Toby and smiled. "Come give me a hug too."

Toby ran to her, threw his arms around her and Stink.

Moss joined in the group hug. Everyone was crying and Jesse was barking and jumping up and down.

Without breaking the embrace, Stink turned his face to Mira and smiled. "We accept the challenge."

***

Eisenstein took two steps back. Feral instinct told him the woman who had suddenly appeared behind Mister Gates was not one to be taken lightly. The fear coursing through his veins made it feel as if his blood had caught fire.

Avram fell back with the others where they gathered close together like crows on a tree limb.

"I thought you killed her," Eisenstein whispered to Mira.

"I thought so too." She stood stoic and statuesque, though seeing Cassandra Gates had shocked her to her core. The old crippled woman, so easy to kill in her wheelchair, now stood barefoot not ten feet away. She wore that same blue flannel nightdress she had on when Mira had killed her. The hole punched in its middle from the wrist fang was clearly visible, and the blood that had spilled from the wound still stained the light blue material. However, the gown was badly ripped and soiled, front and back, and her feet were cut and skinned up to her ankles. It looked as if she had run all the way from Wichita, the entire one-hundred-fifty miles.

Mira had seen many incredible events in her life. This had to have been in the top three, right after the births of her sons. Still, she had no fear of Cassandra Gates. Mira had killed her once, she'd kill her again.

As dawn began to defuse light on the horizon, she had it figured that this would be her finest hour.

***

Toby had never felt so helpless. He was about to stand by and let his momma faceoff against Mira Lawrence in a battle that would determine the fate of Protection, but there had to be a way to call off the challenge.

"I protest," Toby shouted to Eisenstein and Mira.

"What's a protest?" Eisenstein asked.

"My brother didn't think this through before he accepted the challenge. Our momma isn't dead, so Mira Lawrence ain't wanted for her murder no more. We have nothing to gain and everything to lose. I want to call off the challenge."

"You can't do that."

"Why not?"

"If you do, Mira wins by default and Protection is ours."

"That's not fair."

"Sounds like a personal problem."

"Son of a bitch!"

Cassandra put her dainty hand on Toby's shoulder. "Everything is going to be all right." Dark veins slithered through her chalk-white skin just below her collarbones, spread along her neck on both sides, up her throat, and webbed out under her jaw.

He stepped back. "Momma, you can't do this."

"When you boys went to war, I worried each and every time the phone rang. And I could do nothing about whatever fate had in store for you. I was powerless to help you boys, the most important things in my life."

"But we made it home, Momma."

"And I thought my torment was over, but then I lost the use of my legs, and I felt powerless again, like God was testing me, but that alone wasn't enough. He took Moss's leg as well and let loose his personal demons that made a normal life for him and me impossible." She fixed her gaze right into Toby's eyes. "But I am not powerless now. I am the furthest thing from powerless I've ever been. I'm not sure how the winds of fate have turned in this direction, but those winds are now blowing strong and directly against my back."

Jesse whined at Momma's feet.

"But Mira's powerful and she's fast and she's mean as a snake."

"What will it be?" Mira shouted. "Fight or forfeit?"

"Forget the challenge, Mira." Talbot stepped from the shadows. "It won't bring Evan back."

"Stay out of this, Talbot."

He stepped around and faced Mira, his back to Cassandra and the others. "Please. Let's go home."

"You sicken me, Talbot. Why would you have me go back to the shadows when we could have an entire town? We could make a new world for ourselves filled with art and music and theater. Your mind is as small as your poems."

Talbot shook off the slight. He knew she was just peeved. "It's not where we live that matters, in a mansion, in the shadows, in a cardboard box. It's how we live, Mira. In our hearts, in our minds, in our souls. I love you."

"You're a foolish man."

"I just want you to come home with me, safe and unharmed."

A smile took over her lips. "Of that you have nothing to fear, my love." She looked at Cassandra. "The challenge stands."

"No, Mira, please."

"Step aside, Talbot."

"I beg you—"

She drove an open palm into the center of his chest and sent him flying backwards to land in a heap on the ground in front of the others.

"I'll take care of this as I always have." She looked down at Talbot. "There's only one way this can end."

Light, low in the sky announced a new day was about to dawn.

She stepped around Talbot and faced Cassandra, feet spread, arms out at her sides, palms forward. Sharp black fangs shot out of her wrists. "I say we fight. More fun that way."

"Boys," Cassandra shouted. "Everyone, stay back,"

Jesse started a deep growl.

Mira smiled. A red glow of evil flashed in her eyes. "As you said, Mrs. Gates, family is indeed everything. What I do now is for my family and my clan."

Cassandra braced herself, took the same position

as Mira and flicked her wrists. Nothing happened. She tried again. No bone, no fang, no weapon. Nothing. She stepped back.

Mira cackled. "You make this so easy—"

Her eyes popped open wide. She halted in mid-breath. Her arms shot out to her sides and froze in mid-air. She dropped her head and stared down at a long, pointed sword sticking out from the center of her chest. The blade was streaked with her own blood.

"Huh..." She looked up, her eyes flooded with confusion.

The blade pulled free. Mira staggered. The blade sang through the air and sliced horizontally through her neck. Her body crumpled to the parking lot as her head bounced along the ground and stopped face-down in the dirt gutter.

Cassandra held her breath, Toby and Stink too, and everyone else as they watched Tagawa step forward. "It's my house."

"Father." Kasumi rushed to embrace him.

The bright yellow orb of the rising sun broke over the horizon, casting long shadows across Bubs' Place.

Toby pivoted the Alaskan, expecting an attack, but every single Walchok was gone.

Chapter 33

TOBY STOOD IN HIS PARENTS' kitchen and took another swallow of Boulevard lager. His thigh wound throbbed some, but Doc had plucked out all the buckshot and wrapped it up good. Toby had to wear loose-fitting camo cargo pants instead of his jeans. Other than that, he was good to go.

He watched his mother prepare hamburger for the grill. She pressed the raw ground meat together in her hands until she had perfectly rounded patties. Then with a smile she carefully placed each one on a tray lined with wax paper.

"There." She stepped back and admired her handiwork as if she'd just created a great work of art.

"How are you feeling, Momma?" He took a swig of his beer.

She glanced at him over her shoulder. "Better every day."

He gritted his teeth. She didn't look better, still anemic according to Doc, her skin pallid and translucent enough to reveal red and blue blood vessels beneath the surface. Sickly to the point of spooky. Her hair lacked its usual luster and hung to her shoulders like shredded newspaper. However, she could walk again and she was alive, and those things were more important than her looks. "It's good to see you back home with Moss. Been a long time."

"That place in Wichita was just..."

"Forget about that place, Momma."

"...boring," she finished. "I'm happy to be home with my boys...just hope you're not going off to any new wars."

"Stink and I ain't going nowhere."

She wiped her hands with a dishtowel and hugged him around his middle. "I'm not going anywhere either, son."

Toby felt the wiry strength in her arms and didn't want to let her go when she pulled away and turned back to the cook-top range. She'd always loved to cook, and that hadn't changed. She loved to eat, too, but Toby hadn't seen her eat a morsel since she'd come back to Protection. Maybe that was a side effect of once being dead.

Sounds of the Chiefs' game came from the TV in

the front room, and the occasional cheers and groans from Moss and Stink who were watching the game, along with Emma Naveed. Stink had invited over. They sat together on the couch with her head nestled into the crook of his arm. What an odd couple they made, living proof that *opposites attract*.

Moss occupied his usual easy chair, his crutch propped up within reaching distance. He seemed contented now that Momma was home. Maybe now he could accept the loss of his leg, think of it as a challenge and not a handicap, and be his own man again. He'd certainly proven his worth against the Walchoks.

Lilly lay by the potbelly stove in the corner, soaking up the warmth and ignoring the goings-on. If dogs missed their owners, Toby couldn't tell by this one. She seemed as happy to be here as anywhere.

Dirt pelted the window glass behind him. He moved to the back kitchen window and gazed outside. It was an unusually warm Sunday afternoon for early December, and the sun filtered through the trees Momma had planted along the edge of the yard twenty years ago. Since he was a kid, this backyard was where his momma spent countless spring and summer days, feeding birds, rabbits and squirrels, and digging in her flower and vegetable gardens.

Right now, Jesse was doing the digging. Loose soil flew into the air in high arcs, some hitting the side of the house fifty feet from the dig site.

"Stupid dog." Toby set his Boulevard lager on the kitchen counter, glanced at his momma, totally engrossed in making a pie, and headed out the back door. He stepped across the patio and onto the winter-brown lawn. The late-afternoon sun warmed his face as he scanned the wide yard. As far back as he could remember, it wasn't unusual to see local wildlife scampering about. There were always rabbits in the yard, and ground hogs and gophers nosing through the grass. Kansas was flush with these rodents, but today there were none that he could see. It had been six months since his momma was here, six months since she'd put out food for the animals. They'd probably just stopped coming around, and judging from the peanuts and crackers and carrot sticks scattered in the grass, he figured the animals would be back as soon as word got around that Momma was home.

Another barrage of dirt flew out of the hole Jesse was digging. A backhoe couldn't have done a better job. Toby marveled at the little dog's strength and speed. The creature had somehow transferred its healing properties and strength to Jesse when it slashed him. Doc Barnett was stumped, and Toby wondered if Frank Rinaldi had any of these curious aftereffects from the thigh wound Mira had inflicted on him with her wrist fang. That wouldn't surprise Toby one bit.

He strode to the hole and stopped among irregular piles of dirt, some as high as his knees. He dared a look down inside the hole where Jesse dug furiously with his front paws. It would take Toby hours of backbreaking work to shovel the dirt back into the hole. "Jesse, cut it out."

The dog responded with another shower of dirt.

"Toby," came a familiar voice from the back door. He turned to see Kasumi standing on the porch. She looked naked without her sword, and beautiful with the setting sun aglow on her face. The long wool coat made her look New York City stylish.

"You made it." Toby started toward her. He remembered thinking she might have been the sister he never had. Those thoughts did not gel the same now. Maybe someday she could be the girlfriend he never had. "Did your dad come too?"

She hugged him, something he hadn't expected. "He's not the same man he used to be, always smiling."

"Momma too."

"And he's obsessed with those stupid traps."

"He shouldn't need them anymore."

"He's set them all around the property outside, checks them every hour, says he can't leave them, not even to come here for dinner. I don't know what to think."

"Momma's cooking all the time, must have something to do with what they'd been through, being murdered and all."

"Haya won't even talk to Sho, says he's a ghost." Kasumi looped an arm around Toby's waist. "Let's go in. Sheriff Lockwood and Doc brought me. They're inside. Your mother is already setting places for them at the table."

"I better get busy grilling those burgers then."

"I'll help you."

He started the propane grill, and then led her back inside. Momma was peeling potatoes, an entire twenty-five pound bag of them. Toby let her have her little pleasures and passed her without saying a word. Kasumi stopped to give her a hand.

In the front room, Lockwood stood by the door. Doc already found a place next to Emma on the couch. He'd set his cowboy hat on the lampshade. Lilly, tail wagging, set her nose on Doc's knee and was getting a petting.

Moss was watching the Chiefs kick Denver's ass. An air-raid siren couldn't have distracted him.

"Sheriff, help yourself." Toby indicated the cushy chair across the room.

"Thanks, I'll stand."

"Want a beer?"

"I'm good."

"Take your coat?"

"Sure." Lockwood peeled off his bomber jacket. "Closet couldn't be here. He's still recovering from his wounds. LaVertis hasn't left his side."

Doc said, "Go ahead, Reid, tell them."

"Tell us what?" Stink asked.

"Okay." Lockwood cleared his throat. "Officially, Mayor Lawrence and his wife have decided to remain in Boliva indefinitely. Talbot has resigned as mayor of Protection. Doc is going to fill in until the next election."

Stink reached across Emma's body and offered Doc a beefy handshake. "Congratulations, Mayor Barnett."

"Me too." Toby saluted him.

Emma smiled. "You'll make a good mayor, Doc."

"Thanks."

Moss couldn't have cared less.

"Mister Eisenstein claimed Mira's body,"

Lockwood went on. "We had her listed as Jane Doe in the morgue, something Dr. Collins wouldn't have allowed, but he's in Tucson, so what he doesn't know won't piss him off."

"What about Avram?" Toby was sure he'd be a problem. "Once a thug, always a thug."

"I don't know about him," Lockwood said. "He should be with the rest of them holed up in Dodge City. Eisenstein promised me there'd be no further conflict with the Walchoks. They just want to be left in peace, so I'm not going after Avram for the murder of Ben Guralnick. We've been through that once with Mira. I don't want to go through it again. Officially, Ben fell, broke his neck, no coroner here to dispute it, we'll bury him tomorrow. You're all invited to the funeral."

"Sit down and watch the game," Moss said.

"I'll get my beer." Toby stepped into the kitchen. Kasumi wasn't there. Momma was frying potatoes. He picked up his beer from the counter and went to the back door. Kasumi was standing at the grill, coat off, apron on, and hamburgers under her watchful eye. Jesse was sitting at her feet, all excited about what she was doing. He was dirty from head to tail and in dire need of a bath. That would be for another day. Toby wanted to go out on the patio with them, but since Kasumi had everything under control, he went back to the front room.

Before long, Momma came in with a plate: hamburger, fried potatoes, baked beans. "Supper's ready." She handed the plate to Moss, knowing he'd starve before he'd get up from watching the game.

The seven of them sat around the dining room table, elbow to elbow, cozy as could be. Buns and burgers were passed around.

Emma said grace.

Lockwood fixed his plate. He was surprised that Emma was here, that Stink had asked her to join his family and friends for dinner, especially since his mother had theoretically just come back from the dead. If theirs was a budding romance, Lockwood's position on the paranormal being real would have been proven beyond any doubt. If Ben was still alive, he would have agreed.

Toby glanced at Kasumi more than once. He'd only taken a single bite of his hamburger, and now he was pushing baked beans around on his plate with his butter knife. Something was on that boy's mind. If Ben were here he'd know what it was. Toby wasn't even drinking his beer.

Cassandra was the real puzzler of the Gates bunch. She sat straight and motionless in her chair at the end of the table closest to the sink. No plate or utensils in front of her, she just sat in silence with a glass of water in her hand and gazed at her dinner companions. If it weren't for the intricate web of dark veins creeping up her neck and under her jaw, the smile on her face might have been warm and comforting. If Dr. Collins was in town, he'd recommend a check up, thinking she'd contracted some morbid illness. Lockwood knew illness had nothing to do with her condition, but why she wasn't eating with her guests remained a mystery.

Stink would flicker his eyes in Emma's direction; he looked like a moose in heat, but she didn't seem to mind his flirtatious attentions. If she knew what was really going on with this family, she'd get on a bus for Kansas City and never look back.

He sighed. At least the family was together again, and that was all that mattered.

***

After dinner, Toby started his second trip to the kitchen sink with dirty dishes in his hands. He wanted to say something to his momma as he walked by her, still sitting at the table; he wanted to at least offer her a smile, but he couldn't even force one. The woman who had raised him and Stink with kindness and wisdom now seemed but a hulk of her former self. Sure, she was smiling, going through the motions of being normal, but she was back from the dead, goddamn it. That wasn't normal in anybody's book, so how could their lives be normal from here on out? No wonder he couldn't shake that tingle between his shoulder blades.

Moss was asleep in the chair, the empty plate askew in his lap. In the end, the Broncos had bloodied the Chiefs, and he had no reason to remain conscious. Toby took the plate away.

Stink bent to Momma in her chair and kissed her doughy cheek. "I'm taking Emma home now."

"So nice to meet you, Emma." Cassandra smiled that molasses sweet smile.

"Y-you too, ma'am," Emma stammered.

Toby doubted she'd ever be back to this house. Moments later, the Roadmaster tore out of the dirt driveway and barreled down the road toward Protection's town center.

Lockwood got into his bomber jacket. Doc put on his hat. Kasumi handed Toby her long wool coat, and he slipped it over her shoulders for her. It appeared she had inadvertently brought out the gentleman in him. Would miracles ever cease?

"Call me," she said and left with the two men.

He was hoping for another hug, but that didn't happen. Then it suddenly occurred to him that he was alone with Momma. Maybe he should ask her why she didn't eat a bite at dinner. Was she hungry? What was death like? How does it feel to be alive again? Was there anything he could do for her? He settled on the latter question, just to keep the conversation from getting too personal. After all, life after death...a conversation couldn't get more personal than that.

In the kitchen, she stood at the sink, washing dishes and smiling as if there was nothing more delightful in the world.

"Is there anything I can do for you?" Toby asked.

"Sure, dear. You can take out the trash."

He stepped to the garbage can. The bag was full. He pulled it out, twisted it closed, and strode out the back door.

It was cool enough outside to require a coat, and the sky showed only a dim glow where the sun had set behind the trees. The cold air of a typical December night would return very soon.

He flipped the switch for the patio light.

Jesse jumped out of his excavation project, trotted to Toby, and stopped at his feet. The dog's tail wagged so fast it was a blur. Toby smiled, bent to the dog, and patted his side. "Look at you, Jesse. You're a mess." He should hose down the dog right now, get him good and cold; that'd teach him to dig holes in the yard.

Jesse stood on his hind legs and stretched his filthy front paws against Toby's leg. "You're getting mud on me." Oh well. Toby scratched Jesse's head. Heck. His recent ferocious digging aside, the sight of the little mutt so happy, and obviously in good health, was the one thing that brought a smile to Toby's heart. As always, when good-hearted Jesse was around, the world seemed a much better place. Tomorrow he'd get a nice warm bath with lots of doggie shampoo. "How does that sound, boy?"

He barked.

Toby lifted the lid on one of the large metal trashcans beside the patio.

Jesse growled, his nose pointed at the trashcan.

"What is it, boy?" Toby glanced inside. The light wasn't the greatest to see by, but it was enough to reveal what looked like a ball of fur, or a fur hat...no, a dead animal. What the hell? He reached in, pinched the fur between his fingers, and lifted out a...The ears were long, like a rabbit's ears, but the body was flattened, like everything had been sucked out of it.

"Shit." He dropped the shriveled carcass and the garbage bag and staggered backward. All the breath escaped his lungs as if he'd been kicked in the balls.

A thousand hot blades stabbed at his brain.

Now he knew why Momma didn't eat a bite at dinner. Momma had already fed. And he understood full well why Tagawa was obsessed with setting his traps around the Darabont estate. He had to eat too.

Toby squeezed his eyes shut, trying to erase the twisted image of how that poor rabbit had met its demise. Momma fed it, trapped it, and killed it. How could he explain this to Stink and Moss?

Momma was the monster now.

Chapter 34

TALBOT'S FINGERS CLENCHED the steering wheel of the Chevy Avalanche he'd found parked in Eisenstein's driveway. The keys were left in the ignition. He started the engine and backed out into the street. Mira's funeral was on his mind, a morbid affair: closed casket, her head set where it should have been attached to her neck, black roses, and a thirty-four piece orchestra. He'd finally treated her to a taste of the arts she'd missed so much.

Lately, nobody in the clan had paid him much attention. He'd lost his wife. Ephram had lost his mother. He'd lost his job. Their world in the shadows had become a nightmare of its own.

The sun had just set, and the last streaks of daylight would disappear in a few minutes. Each day since her death, from the moment he awoke to the instant he collapsed into bed at night, he had tried to ignore the unrelenting pressure at the back of his head, the ache in his heart born from the tears of his son. He was now a fine-looking boy: thin boned, handsome boyish face, blond hair combed down over his forehead. Mira would never get to know him.

Talbot put the transmission into drive. He had always been one to turn the other cheek when slapped in the face, to make love not war. He had always been softhearted. Mira had been the true strength of their family, which had left him to his poetry and his minuscule duties as Protection's mayor. Tagawa had changed all that.

Now Mira was gone, killed, murdered like Evan was murdered, and what was the clan's position on his personal tragedy?

A truce.

Eisenstein had explained why the abrupt truce with the folks of Protection was a good idea. It was an old argument, one Mira fought fervently, that exposure could lead to government intrusion, military conflict, and eventual imprisonment and possible extermination. They had to keep a low profile to survive, but in the end, she was right. What kind of life was living in the shadows? Ephram deserved more than obscurity. Evan too. He could have been President of the United States if given half a chance.

Talbot fiddled with the radio dial until *Eye of the Tiger* blared from the speakers.

Sho Tagawa had paid for his crime with his life, but through some merciless quirk of fate or physics, he'd come back to life, as did Cassandra Gates. Talbot knew her death was Toby Gates' punishment for nearly killing him with that big gun of his. The attack had come unexpectedly, as he'd just told the Gates boys to go home.

For that they were both going to pay dearly. Talbot now knew better than to stab humans with his fang. They'd just come back to life with all the powers he possessed. No, turnabout was fair play. They would all lose their heads for what they had done to Mira.

Starting with Toby Gates.

Talbot pressed hard on the accelerator and sped away from Eisenstein's refuge in Dodge City, the headlights aimed directly toward Protection, Kansas.

About the Author

Over the years, Lane has published numerous short stories. His most recent is *Best's Laid Plans*, in which The Beatles original drummer, Pete Best, travels back in time to prevent being fired by The Beatles and replaced by Ringo. *Bests' Laid Plans* appeared in Electric Spec magazine. Other works: *Anthem*, a road-trip comedy in which a man is challenged to sing the national anthem at all 30 major-league baseball parks within 60 days; *Below Par*, where a young man goes from non-golfer to a touring pro within nine months; and *Under the Rim, Beneath the Goalposts, and Into the Dirt*, a non-fiction narrative compilation of the incredibly stupid off-the-field antics of basketball, football, and baseball players. Lane is a lawyer and lives in Parker, Colorado with his wife, Barbara, three horses: BLT, Gus, and Dallas, his dog Ollie, and Cady, his fascinating barn cat.

Enjoy more short stories and novels from
TWB Press

http://www.twbpress.com